Murder by Magic

D1413421

Edmund jr ...

Cranberry Country Mysteries:

Murder by Magic

Murder in an Old, Dark House

Murder on a Lonely Bog

Murder at Anawan Rock

Marmalade and Murder

Murder by Magic

A Cranberry Country Mystery

by

Edward Lodi

ROCK VILLAGE PUBLISHING

Middleborough, Massachusetts

FIRST PRINTING

ISBN 978-1-934400-47-0

Rock Village Publishing
41 Walnut Street
Middleborough MA 02346
(508) 946-4738
rockvillage@verizon.net

CONTENTS

Murder by Magic

PROLOGUE

The Secret

CHAPTER I

Into the Night

Ross Ashley stepped off the pavement and into the woods.

As his feet sank into the leaf mold he caught a glimpse of the moon, high above the treetops, drifting among the stars like a cast-off nail paring. A mere sliver, it provided scant light—just enough glow for him to see where to place one foot before the other without falling flat on his face; enough for a shaky advance, like a post-operative patient allowed out of bed for the first time.

A moment later, sliding behind a clot of clouds, the moon denied him even that miserly allotment, leaving him enveloped in stygian darkness. The clouds, which had been gathering since early evening, threatened rain: heavy, prolonged rain. Not for a while, though. He should have ample time before the rain began for what he had to do. And if not enough time…well, he would get wet.

It was safe now to use the flashlight. He swept its beam low against the ground, in a wide semicircle, until it showed the path which would guide him through the swamp to the cranberry bog. After the bog the going would be easier. The dirt track along the side of the bog led, eventually, to the first of the fields he needed to cross in order to reach the farmhouse. Ross knew the area well; he had traversed it many a time—though always by day—while hunting. Tonight he was once again on the hunt. But not for game. He carried no gun. He carried with him, besides the flashlight, an empty canvas sack.

If his hunt proved successful, the sack would be full upon his return.

Most likely, though—he had to be honest with himself—the sack would remain empty.

Somewhere an owl hooted, a muted cry, like the faint whistle of a distant train. Or perhaps it was just that, a train, a freight on its way to Boston or Cape Cod. There were other sounds too. The tread of his feet against dry leaves. The whisper of the wind through bare branches. The banshee shriek of a dead tree as, leaning, it rubbed against a live neighbor whenever the wind gusted.

Although it was November the swamp teemed with life. He could smell its rich pungency: rotting vegetation; earthworms churning the leaf mold into soil; pink salamanders curled in shallow cavities under stones and logs; fat grubs gorging on decay. He could see in his mind's eye turkeys roosting on tree limbs, chipmunks lodged in crevices, woodchucks tucked in tight for the winter in their underground burrows, deer hunkered down for the night, coyotes on the prowl.

He smiled at his folly for having ventured out on such a night, in pursuit of what? A chimera. A will-o'-the-wisp. But then, had he not always, since childhood, inhabited a world made up of dreams?

Was what he now found himself in a dream? or a nightmare?

The path Ross followed was a well-worn animal trail, made more pronounced by hunters like himself, and the occasional berry picker or bird watcher: just enough traffic to keep the way free of briars and other bothersome vegetation, like poison ivy.

Of the latter there was plenty, off to either side, mostly stripped of leaves now, but recognizable to one familiar with the woods.

He picked his way cautiously. He was on higher ground now. Obligatory for a rural New England landscape, a stone wall ran parallel to the path. Some early settler, as far back as the seventeenth century perhaps, had cleared this end of the swamp and marked it off with rocks and boulders laboriously pried loose and rolled, carried, or dragged on sleds to the boundaries. Ross would encounter many such walls before reaching the farmhouse. In his childhood the old-timers, the swamp Yankees from whom he was partly descended (the others who swung from the branches of his family tree were Portuguese and Irish), used to say, "These damn fields ain't nothin' but bones," meaning stones of course, but actual bones too he thought, thinking of the land and its storied past, the Wampanoags and the Pilgrims, the plagues the English brought with them, the bitter legacy of King Philip's War.

A long time ago, long before the Civil War, many of the pastures and croplands were abandoned, the owners gone west, or to the cities; after their defection the woodlands crept back, blotted out the fields. Only the stone walls remained, and here and there a paddock or a pound, a cellar hole, a forgotten well, an overgrown gravestone or two to show that the land had once been farmed, had once been a place where people lived loved fought and died.

Not everyone had deserted New England or the countryside. Some stayed put. For example the Hickmans. The Hickmans were among those flint-hard Yankees who for reasons known only to themselves adhered to the land, as if mired up to their knees in it: adhered to it throughout the nineteenth century, ignoring the siren calls of Westward Expansion, Manifest Destiny, the California Gold Rush. On into the twentieth century, indifferent to two world wars or the Great Depression in between. Maybe their fields were a bit more fertile than those of their neighbors. Less bony. Or maybe it was just that the Hickmans were a bit more stubborn than the folks around them. Or lazier. Less ambitious, less adventuresome. Maybe the thought of heading West in a Conestoga wagon breathing dust through Indian territory didn't appeal to them, or rounding Cape Horn in a tall ship buffeted by storms to face an uncertain future in an unknown land. Maybe they preferred life on their hardscrabble farm, against all odds just barely making ends meet, preferred that to city life toiling twelve hours a day, six days a week in a grim factory, breathing the soot of polluted air.

Or maybe it was something else. The Secret.

CHAPTER II
Old Joe

All he had to go on was an old man's demented fantasy. An old man lying flat on his back in a nursing-home bed, scarcely breathing, straining to hear, at his door, the faint rat-a-tat-tat of death's dry knuckles.

"It shoulda been mine," Joe said, in a rare moment of lucidity. "They stole it from me." His gnarled fingers gripped his hand. "You take it. You been good to me. You can have it. It won't do me no good, here, in this shit hole."

In any event Joe was not your typical Hickman. "Hick may be the first part of my name," he said more than once, with a sour grin, exhaling sour breath, "but I ain't no hick."

One day out of the blue he began to explain his wanderings: "My old man dragged me out to the shed with a birch rod one time too many. I don't remember what it was for, not that it would have made no difference. Some stupid thing I did or didn't do, or just because he was in an ornery mood and hadn't beat me in the last couple days and needed some way to fill his time.

"But like I say it was one time too many. I was just a kid, a scrawny kid at that, but I hauled off and let him have it, bare-fisted, square in the kisser. Near to broke my knuckles." He laughed at the memory, mirthlessly, through toothless gums.

"I caught the sonofabitch off guard. You should of seen the dazed look his eyes took before his knees buckled and he went down like a felled ox. When he picked hisself off the floor he was foaming at the mouth, like a rabid dog, blood dripping down his split lip. For a long while he just stood there, shaking hisself, like he was dizzy and had to clear away the cobwebs. Then he up and took a wild lunge at me. He'd of kilt me then and there with his bare hands if he had've got a hold of me.

"But I was too fast for him. I seen what was coming and lit outa there like a cat with its tail on fire." He chuckled. "That was the last time I ever seen him, or Ma, or any of 'em. The only one of the bunch I ever kept in touch with after that was Molly."

So, at the age of fourteen Joe Hickman ran away from the family farmstead and took to the open road, to see the country, to roam the world. He worked at whatever jobs came his way. At one time or another he was a circus roustabout, a railroad gandy dancer, an oyster pirate on Long Island Sound, a hobo when need be, a doughboy in World War I.

Joe fought in the trenches in France, escaped being gassed or blown to bits with shrapnel but not being shot in the thigh by a sniper, one night when he struck a match to light a cigarette. His wounds were not fatal, just serious enough to earn him a modest pension for life. Joe returned to the States, performed odd jobs for the rest of his working life, never married or settled down, and ended up, at the age of eighty-five, in the Swallows Rest Nursing Home in Wareham, where he shared a room with Ross Ashley's grandfather. Which is how Ross came to know him.

Ross visited his granddad faithfully, once a week. His Grand-pa Ashley didn't have much to say on those visits, he'd withdrawn into himself, and remained withdrawn up until the time he died, so to while away the time Ross got in the habit of talking to Joe Hickman instead. Joe still had his faculties then, or most of them. He'd led an interesting life, had stories to tell, never the same one twice, but no one to listen to him tell them, except for Ross, and a nurse or two who humored him. Ross didn't humor him. Ross was genuinely interested.

Especially when Joe hinted of secrets. Things he'd heard, or sensed, when he was a boy and still living at the farm. Secrets his sister Molly shared with him over the years, in their infrequent correspondence by letter.

When Ross's grandfather finally died, after two and a half years, Ross kept up his weekly visits to the nursing home. He'd grown fond of old Joe. And of his secrets.

CHAPTER III
The Farmhouse

He was out of the swamp now, and beyond the cranberry bog, into the first of the fields that lay between him and the farmhouse. This one must have once enclosed livestock; its stone wall was higher than most, three feet, but easily surmounted by a young man in his prime. The field was overgrown with tall weeds turned brittle and sere, dotted here and there with stunted red cedar and white pine saplings, and clumps of sumac, especially along the wall.

No longer sheltered by the thick growth of the swamp Ross Ashley shivered at the wind's cold breath as it explored the edges of his jacket, seeking entry for itself and the rain that was to come.

Who was the greater fool, he wondered. The old man? Or Ross Ashley?

Joe Hickman, with his long-guarded family secrets, which might be nothing more than his, or someone else's, fantasies or lies? Or Ross Ashley, credulous enough to venture forth late at night through rough terrain in the face of an impending nor'easter, with no basis for doing so other than the maunderings of a demented old man?

He must be a damn fool, he thought, if for no other reason than that he had chosen a roundabout route fraught with obstacles and pitfalls to reach a deserted farmhouse which in daylight he could have easily, and without risk to life or limb, accessed by paved road. But then, he was a self-confessed romantic, wasn't he? A dreamer, a weaver of fantasies: not a hell of a lot different from the demented old man.

He had, judging by the number of stone walls he'd encountered, arrived at the last field. Or had he? The night was pitch black. He had relied on his familiarity with the terrain, more than on the pinprick of light the flashlight gave off, to guide him. Perhaps he'd been walking around in circles, had jumped over the same stone wall twice, maybe three times.

No. He wasn't lost; he trusted his innate sense of direction, his knowledge of the lay of the land. He should be coming upon the farmhouse soon. That is, if he didn't snag his foot on a briar first and break a leg, or blunder into an abandoned well.

And lo! What he'd taken for a bank of clouds hanging low in the sky proved to be the farmhouse in silhouette, no more than a hundred feet ahead. He chuckled to himself. The old place was rumored to be haunted—probably the reason why vandals hadn't trashed it, or set it ablaze on Halloween. That, and its isolated position. Hunters like himself respected it as private property, no matter that the town had long ago seized the estate for nonpayment of taxes. Respected it, even though the house was slowly rotting into the ground, as was the barn, and most of the outbuildings. Of the barn only a pile of collapsed boards and shingles remained, a jumbled heap of rubble overgrown with brambles and vines, like the burial mound of some ancient civilization, deep in the jungle, swallowed up eons ago by encroaching vegetation.

Ross Ashley stood before the farmhouse and stared, and wondered if it was, after all, haunted.

Well, for one tired, worn-out old man it certainly was. Its ghosts, whether real or imagined, still tormented Joe Hickman.

He'd fled the place at the tender age of fourteen, black sheep of the family, disgraced, disowned, disinherited, leaving his old life behind, not only his abusive father, but his mother and siblings as well. He never saw any of them again, alive, although he claimed that Molly visited him regularly at Swallows Rest, at night, always alone—Molly, still a skinny knock-kneed twelve-year-old, the age she'd been the day he left for good, the only one of his half dozen brothers and sisters with whom he'd communicated, by letter, sporadically, over the decades he was away.

According to Joe Molly had died, unmarried, in her late seventies, but when she came to see him at the nursing home in the cramped room he shared with a four-hundred-and fifty-pound diabetic eight of whose toes had been amputated she was a bare-foot, pig-tailed little girl, wearing the same tattered pink hand-me-down dress she'd had on the last time he saw her, that day in 1904, when he'd cold-cocked his father in the wood shed, and like Huckleberry Finn lit out for the territories.

Not that old Joe Hickman had ever read Mark Twain. It was for romantics like Ross Ashley to read adventure classics, men like Ross who Peter Pan-like had never quite mastered the skill of growing up, who in adulthood still dreamed of pirates and buried treasure, who were gullible enough to take seriously the ramblings of a demented old man.

The wind intensified. He heard it howling through the trees, in the swamp he'd left behind, beyond the cranberry bog. Or if howling was too strong a word, moaning. He could hear the wind moaning through the trees. It would begin to rain soon. A sensible man would have driven his car down the paved road, turned into the dirt track that led to the farmhouse, parked in the clearing, done what he'd come for, and been home by now. But Ross Ashley was not a sensible man. If he were, he would have stayed home in the first place.

Molly Hickman had died some five years ago. Other than her reprobate brother, she was the last of her clan. The last, anyhow, that Ross knew about. If any of the other siblings, or their descendants, were still alive they hadn't stepped forward to save the old homestead from decay and foreclosure, hadn't offered to pay the back taxes owed to the town. And with luck hadn't, as old Hickman insisted, been privy to The Secret.

"Molly was the only one of us bunch Ma ever trusted," he whispered to Ross one afternoon, when the two-toed mound of flesh in the next bed was, apparently, snoozing—though one never knew. He might be listening. They had only his stertorous breathing, and the arrhythmic churnings and seismic upheavals of his ponderous chest beneath the coverings, as proof that he was asleep.

"The son of a bitch might be faking," the old man pointed out, though Ross seriously doubted whether the unfortunate diabetic (who was probably only in his mid forties, and of dubious intellectual capacity) could be that good an actor. It sounded as if each breath of air he took might well be his last.

"Just hope he don't fart," Hickman said. "He does that sometime. Farts in his sleep." He made a show of compressing his nose between two fingers. "Stinks to high heaven." He shook his head, as if to rid himself of the memory. "Something wicked this way comes! You ain't smelled nothing till you've smelled one of that fellow's farts." He paused, as if pondering the magnitude of his roommate's flatulence.

15

After a while he said: "I miss your grandpappy. A skinny man like him, he just picked at his food. What little bit he ate, he hardly farted at all. And when he did, they didn't stink, anyhow not so as you'd notice."

Old man Hickman had then grown silent again, lying on his raised bed with eyes closed, head propped on the pillow, lost in thought, or just letting his mind wander. Ross sat by his side, ready to get up and leave if the old man fell asleep.

Hickman opened his eyes. "He's only got two toes, you know," he said finally.

"So you told me."

"They cut the other eight off."

"Yes."

"It drives me crazy, wondering."

"About what?"

"Where is his two toes, the two they didn't slice off, located? Has he got one on each foot? Or is the both of them on one and the same foot? And if that's the case, which foot?"

At a loss for words, Ross had merely shrugged, then said, to humor the old man: "And then the additional question arises, which toes are they, and how are they positioned? The big toe and the little toe at the far ends, with nothing in between? Two middle toes? Or…the possible combinations are endless."

Old man Hickman contemplated this, then said: "Do me a favor?"

"Well…" Ross stonewalled. He had an inkling of what was coming. Had, in fact, brought it upon himself, by indulging the old man in his morbid curiosity.

"Take a peek. See where they's at."

"I can't do that, Mr. Hickman. Mr. Cardoza has a right to privacy."

Old man Hickman sighed. "I figured you wouldn't." He

lifted the upper half of his body from the bed and twisted his head toward his roommate. "I never seen anybody so fat."

"Mr. Hickman..."

The old man chuckled. "Don't mind me. I ain't gone off the deep end yet. It's just that I get bored with myself. I ain't used to doing nothing all day. The only visitor I get is you—once a week—and Molly, and she only comes at night when I'm asleep." He smiled sadly, his sunken mouth like a withered Macintosh apple with a slash in its skin. "I know Molly ain't real. But I also believe she is, kinda. Do you think I'm crazy, Ross?"

Ross shook his head. "No. I think Molly is real. To you, and that's what counts."

CHAPTER IV

Folie à Deux

A gout of cold rain smashed against his forehead, wrenching him back to the present. Rain began to pelt other parts of his body too, his ears, his face, his hands: big, tentative drops, harbingers of the torrent that was to follow.

It was time to move on into the house.

The ancient flagstones, paltry and unevenly distributed, that formed the pathway leading up to the house were badly cracked, fragmented, the pieces sunken, the gaps between them where once grass had grown now overtaken by weeds. The porch steps, though rickety, held his weight, as did the floor boards, though these latter sagged and creaked, as if to protest their long neglect.

Ross swung the beam of his flashlight along either side of the front door. The porch was devoid of furniture, as most likely was the house itself. Old man Hickman had said something about an estate sale held by the town, an attempt to recoup some of the taxes owed. This would have been after Molly's death. After the mail carrier had found her, passed out, on the kitchen floor. Molly died a day or two later in the hospital from a combination of ills, mainly heart failure and cancer, just a few short weeks before Hickman, the prodigal son, had taken it upon himself to return to the scene of his abandoned childhood, after six and one-half decades spent ranging the world in search of something,

something intangible, he knew not what, something he could not name nor would have recognized if, against all odds, he had stumbled upon it and stared it stark in the face, had returned home for no special reason, none that he could name, except the obvious, to die.

His timing was off. He'd waited just a tad too long, had assumed that his sister (still in his mind's eye that pigtailed twelve-year-old in a pink hand-me-down dress), two years younger than he, would still be alive and, unlike himself, in robust health. He'd taken a taxi from where the Boston bus had left him off in Middleborough, dismissed the driver and paid her off, with an adequate tip, at the end of the long, lonely drive, to walk in with his lone tattered suitcase and God knows what expectations only to find the place deserted and boarded up.

He'd taken the boards down and moved in. That same night he suffered his first stroke. It was only by chance that town officials, going over the property while making plans for the estate sale, found him, half dead, sprawled on the threshold to the outside, as if in preparing to leave the world he was doing his sister one better, by making it as far as the door.

Other than a week or two in the hospital, old man Hickman had spent the succeeding five years in Swallows Rest with a succession of roommates, every single one of whom had the good sense, sooner or later, to cut short his residence by giving up the ghost, which is how Ross Ashley had come to know Hickman, through his grandfather (whose stint in Swallows Rest as Hickman's roommate had been somewhat longer than the average) and to half believe what the old man himself more than half believed. That is to say, he shared the old man's madness.

The French had a term for it: *folie à deux*.

A type of folly in which one man's lunacy feeds off, and nurtures, the other's. Except maybe it wasn't lunacy after all.

In the meantime the house remained in limbo, the town undecided as to how to proceed, whether to sell, tear down, or simply forget about it and, figuratively, walk away. There had been talk lately, though, reported in the local weekly, that the town was seriously considering allowing the fire department to burn the place down, as a practice exercise, and donating the land to a local conservation group.

If Ross was ever going to prove once and for all whether the old man was delusional or not, the time to act was now.

The front door was locked.

Surprise, surprise. Naturally when the ambulance hauled the old man away the EMTs would have locked it. But would they have bothered with the windows? Or was it a moot question? The place had been boarded up. Had Hickman unlocked any windows, the day of his arrival, when he tore the boards off? Dropping the canvas sack onto the porch floor Ross tried lifting one of the windows with both hands.

He might have saved himself the effort. It was nailed shut. Tight as a bull's ass.

He tried each of the others, with the same result.

By now the rain was beating its fingers in a rhythmic tattoo against the shingled roof. Thwarted by clogged gutters the growing torrents cascaded over the edge. Ross had a choice. He could force entry by smashing, with the aid of the canvas sack, one of the windows and climbing through the broken panes—at the risk of serious injury to himself, including irreparable damage to the family jewels. Or he could try some other window, in another part of the house.

The second option necessitated leaving the shelter of the

porch and getting wet. So what? By the looks of it the rain was here to stay. Sooner or later he would get soaked anyhow, here at the house or on the long walk back over the fields and through the swamp to the secluded spot on the lonely road where he had parked his car.

Tucking the flashlight into the sack he stepped down the rickety steps into the downpour. As he did so he was forcibly reminded of a principle of physics he'd learned in high school: *Water seeks its own level.* As the rain, using his body as a conduit, sought its own level, he cursed himself for a fool.

He went around the house, squeezing behind the shrubbery which, neglected these many years, had grown rampant against the walls: the Japanese quince, the lilacs, the bridal wreaths so beloved of the Victorians, trying each window, without luck. And of course the back door was locked.

He could kick the door in, easily. In the eyes of the law that would constitute breaking and entering. But Ross would feel no guilt. After all, hadn't old man Hickman given him permission to enter the house? True, the house did not legally belong to the old man. But surely, morally he had a claim, as the last of the Hickmans.

Last, except for whatever ghosts might call the old heap home.

If there were ghosts inside they were not being very hospitable—had not, despite the fact that he was standing there getting drenched, invited him in.

Ross Ashley was a law-abiding man. He did not go to church, had not since the age of ten, but he was a man of principles and integrity. He would break in, but only if he had to. He had yet to try the windows on the second floor.

Like many a New England farmhouse whose history spans generations, the Hickman homestead had been added onto numerous times. One of those additions was a lean-to next to the rear entryway, for the storage of firewood. There were stacks of firewood in it even now. Or what had once been firewood, before powder post beetles invaded it and reduced it to sawdust and pulp. There was also a sturdy sawhorse, which the beetles had so far ignored, probably because it had been treated at one time, or had been fashioned from cedar or locust, species of wood which powder post beetles abhor.

Ross dragged the sawhorse out of the lean-to and positioned it in front. He tossed the sack over his head onto the sloped roof, and then stepped onto the sawhorse, where with more luck than skill he maintained a precarious balance on the rain-slick wood, like a cowpuncher rehearsing a rodeo stunt. Teetering, he grasped the overhang and lifted himself up. Scraping his belly against the lip—he bore the bruises for days—he scrambled onto the asphalt shingles. Lying still a moment to gather resolve, he probed with his fingernails for crevices in the shingles, to prevent himself from sliding back, and slowly crawled away from the edge. When he reached the spot where the sack had landed he stood erect.

The water pouring from the sky did nothing to enhance the precarious purchase his shoes had on the steeply pitched roof. One false move and he could find himself sliding toward the edge, or worse, losing his balance, dance a tarantella, and as a grand finale, topple ass over heels onto the ground.

No stranger to the cat-slide roofs common to New England saltboxes, he took comfort in the knowledge that the cant to this lean-to was not nearly as extreme as some he'd seen. So what if the night was pitch-black, the penetrating rain cold, soul-numbing, unrelenting, the roofing slick and treacherous? He might as well proceed to the next level. He would face as much risk of bodily harm by trying to make his way from atop the lean-to back onto terra firma as he would by adhering to the present plan, which was to enter the house through an upstairs window.

The slope of the lean-to was in his favor. At its highest the roof extended all the way up, almost, to the second story. All he had to do was climb as far as the roof went, then stand tippy-toe and—this next part might prove a little dicey—reach up and hope for, first, a window; second, an *unlocked* window; and third, an unlocked window that was not swollen tight from damp, or jammed tight because the house had, over the centuries, settled unevenly.

He was lucky in all respects. Without mishap (other than backsliding half a dozen times, all minor setbacks) he found a window right where he had reasoned one would be. He was able to reach it—just barely. It was unlocked, and though at first reluctant to budge, eventually it allowed itself to be wedged open, enough for him to squeeze through, after having tossed in the empty—save for the flashlight, but soon to be filled, he hoped—canvas sack.

The room he found himself in had once been a bedroom. But with its buckling floorboards littered with bat droppings, its peeling wallpaper streaked with mold, its discolored ceiling beaded with moisture from the porous attic, it could easily pass for a chamber of horrors.

The Hickman House of Horrors. Starring Ross Ashley, in his first and final role.

Something has died here, he thought, choking on the fetid air. *Here or in an adjoining room. A raccoon perhaps.*

He did not pause to investigate but passed quickly through the chamber into the hallway. Ignoring the warren that comprised the upstairs rooms he made his way, with the aid of the flashlight, down the creaking stairs to the first floor. He moved quickly; there were few obstacles to trip him up. As expected, the house like the porch was devoid of furniture. Whatever furnishings and bric-a-brac and what-nots had not sold the day of the sale had evidently been bid on as a lot by a dealer and carted away. The generations of Hickmans who since the early seventeenth century had clung on tenaciously through droughts, Indian wars, revolutions, a civil war, two world wars and any number of depressions had at last passed into oblivion.

Sic transit gloria mundi. Thus passes away the glory of the world.

All but the old man. Joe Hickman. Still alive—albeit rotting in a nursing home bed.

All but the old man and the ghost of the twelve-year-old Molly, who persisted, if only in the old man's mind. And in his— Ross Ashley's.

"I ain't making it up," the old man insisted, the first time he confided the family secret. "Molly told me it herself."

"Molly's dead."

"Told me it in a letter," Hickman snapped impatiently.

"When?"

"Oh, maybe twenty years ago. How the hell am I supposed to remember exactly when? We wrote back and forth all the time, maybe twice a year. I never stayed long in one place. I was always on the move. It was me who wrote the first time, just before World War II, to see if any of the folks was still alive. How could she write to me unless I give her my address?"

"You said yourself she was trying to entice you to come home. She never married. You were the only family she had left. The big brother she hadn't seen since 1904, when she was twelve and you were fourteen. She was lonely. She may have made the whole thing up."

The old man had bent forward in the bed and glared at him. "Molly wouldn't lie. She was the only one of us Hickmans who was decent. Her, and Ma. And Ma wasn't a Hickman, not born as such. She was a Pittsley. It was Pa's blood who tainted us. All of us 'cept for Molly. "

"Do you still have the letter?"

Hickman looked at Ross as if he had two heads. "Don't be a damn fool. You think I'd carry something like that around with me, for prying eyes to see? I didn't keep none of her letters, never mind that one. Her address I kept in my head. The zip code, I mean."

"Did she ever mention it again, after that first time?"

"Lotsa times. In her letters and now when she comes to visit."

Ross chose to ignore that last part.

"And she told you where it's hidden?"

The old man looked at him slyly. "Yep."

Ross knew enough to desist at that point. The old man would tell him where, eventually, in his own good time. Else why would he have mentioned it in the first place?

If the damn thing did indeed exist.

CHAPTER V

Heirloom

If it exists, he thought to himself. *Well, I'll soon know.* He was in the kitchen now. Like the rest of the house it was bare, the worn, scarred, dusty, dirty linoleum on the floor upon which he tread ever so softy (so as not to awaken the ghosts?) the only heirloom left. Even the cast iron sink old man Hickman had described to him was gone, sold for scrap perhaps, or as an antique. One man's trash is another man's treasure.

Speaking of which…

"The cupboard," the old man had whispered, so as not to be overheard. By whom was not apparent. There were no nurses or aids in the room, only Ross and the grossly overweight roommate, the behemoth of a wretch with two remaining toes and an IQ to match.

It was highly unlikely that, eavesdropping and thus learning the secret which over a span of two hundred years successive generations of Hickman patriarchs had kept closely guarded, even from their closest kin, the four-hundred-and fifty-five-pound diabetic would suddenly leap out of bed, shout "Eureka!" and, bouncing out of the room on his two intact toes like a hippo on springs, dash along the corridor and out the door, hobbling on the stubs of his feet, the ends of his hospital johnny flapping in the wind like a funeral shroud tearing loose from a resurrected corpse, hell-bent on being the first to reach the old Hickman homestead and seize possession of what old man Hickman considered rightfully his, though he had no legal claim to it, and a dubious moral one.

"I can't understand why you didn't go to the cupboard first thing," Ross had said. "That's what I would have done."

"Not if you was eighty years old and had spent the last two days traveling by bus from North Carolina and had to change buses in New York City and again in Boston, with hardly nothing to eat and no proper way to sleep. Not if instead of a hot meal and a warm bath and a soft bed you found the house you thought was going to be your home from now on all dilapidated and boarded up and you had to take the boards down all by yourself with some rusty old tools from the shed just so you could get inside and find some kinda clue as to where your little sister was at. I never figured her to be dead," he added sadly. "I was too dog-tired, too hungry and thirsty, too broken-hearted to worry about the cupboard. There wasn't nothing in that house to eat or drink."

So he had fallen asleep with the intention of searching in the morning, but had suffered a stroke instead and by pure chance been discovered the next day and carted off to the hospital, and eventually the nursing home, his place of residence for the past five years, and until the end of time for all he knew.

So it was up to Ross now to retrieve the treasure, if such existed.

The cupboard was where the old man said he would find it, next to where the sink used to be. Ross shone the beam from the flashlight into its interior. The shelves were empty, as he knew they would be, after the estate sale. He let the beam linger, like a lover's fond gaze, on the third shelf. If Molly had told the truth, if old man Hickman wasn't off his rocker, if he—Ross Ashley—wasn't the world's greatest sad-sack sucker, that's where it would be. The Hickman treasure. Behind the false back of the third shelf.

"Just push on the board, hard, that's what Molly writ," Hickman had instructed.

As simple as that.

Ross was tall, the ceiling low, and the cupboard within easy reach. So, laying the flashlight flat on the shelf, he leaned over and with his palms splayed pushed with both hands hard against the false back. The board swung inward, with hardly a protest, on hidden hinges. He picked up the flashlight with his left hand and directed the beam into the aperture he had created, exposing a large, jagged cavity lined with crude bricks.

He picked up the flashlight and shone its beam within.

The cavity was empty.

His pang of disappointment, though keen, was short-lived. "All is not lost," he murmured. He reached inside and probed with his right hand. The cavity was deeper than he had first supposed. He had to stand on tiptoe to reach all the way down to the rough bottom in order to run his fingers along the uneven surface.

Nothing.

Hell, he thought. *There was something in here at one time. There must have been.*

Refusing to admit defeat, he kept probing, inserting his fingers into each tiny crevice. He did this for the next five minutes, running his fingertips over the surface like a blind man reading Braille, gritting his teeth, hoping against hope that there might be a further cavity, a cavity within a cavity, which would turn out to be the treasure's true location.

There was no further cavity.

Even now, even as he scraped his fingers raw, he was rehearsing in his mind what he would say to the old man. Would he tell him the truth? Or would he keep up the fantasy by lying, allowing Hickman to think that there might be a treasure after all.

Dammit. There had to have been. The hidden cavity proved it.

About to withdraw his hand he relaxed his fingers, then on impulse attempted one more probe. And that's when he struck gold. Literally.

He felt it, wedged in a crevice between two bricks where the mortar had been applied unevenly. Whatever it was, it felt both rough and smooth, at the same time. In his attempt to dislodge it he tore the nail of his index finger. Using the blood that dripped from the wound as a lubricant, he worked at freeing the object until, at last, he was able to pry it loose.

He withdrew it slowly. By the feel he knew what it must be before he brought it forth to where, holding it in his palm, he could direct his beam of light upon it: a gold ring, bright and shiny, encrusted with sparkling jewels.

PART ONE

A Winter's Tale

CHAPTER VI
Death Takes a Stroll

Blissfully ignorant of the grim discovery he would make within the hour, Frank Gallerani sat slouched in his favorite chair by the parlor window that overlooked his cranberry bog. As he basked in the warmth cast by the open hearth of the Franklin stove, he was conscious, in equal measure, of the fierce nor'easter raging outside, flakes swirling in eddies, rapidly mounting on the ground just inches away from where he sat safe behind a double pane of sturdy glass; and of his two daughters, Maria and Linda, upstairs in their rooms, working on school projects—or possibly not, if (as was likely) they had been lured away from academic drudgery by the siren call of social media.

The nor'easter slammed into southern New England sometime in the wee hours before dawn; as a consequence the superintendent of Rochester schools had canceled classes for the day. Laura, however, had reported to her job as usual. As head nurse of a large convalescent home and rehabilitation facility, she was obligated to show up for work no matter what. In the blizzard that had paralyzed much of the East a few years back, forewarned by weather forecasts she had hastily packed a few things and gone in a day early, remaining at her post for four consecutive days and nights. Today's storm, though ferocious enough, was a piece of cake in comparison to The Blizzard of '13.

Piece of cake, yes, but with far too much frosting. Roused from his reverie by the thought of the drifting snow that was relentlessly piling up outside, Frank got up from his chair and, with a detour that took him close by the Franklin stove (so that he might carry forth with him the recollection of its warmth), made his way to the mud room off the kitchen. There he donned, for the third time that day, first his boots, then his warm winter jacket, and finally the red woolen hat with its floppy ear flaps that made him, in his own estimation at least, look like a silly jackass, but which had the admitted virtue—besides being a gift from his wife—of truly protecting his ears from the danger of frostbite.

Like a faithful steed inured to the vicissitudes of the New England climate the pickup, with attached plow, stood where he had left it an hour or two earlier at the edge of the gravel apron that bordered the patch of lawn fronting the house. With a brush he swept the snow that had built up in the short while since the last plowing from the windshield and rear and side windows, climbed into the cab, started the engine, and switched the heater to full blast. Within seconds the windows defrosted and he was able to begin scraping away with his plow the nearly three inches of additional snow that had accumulated since his last swipe along the mile-long driveway that led from his house, along the edge of the cranberry bog, by the man-made reservoir that supplied his bog with water, and through the swamp to the paved public road that at last connected him and his family to the rest of the world.

Although the snow was heavy and, in places where it was exposed to the wind, formed deep drifts, the plow cut through it with ease, shoving it aside like shaved ice, his two earlier passes having made this possible. If he did not keep up with the snow, if he let it gather too much, his pickup-cum-plow would be unable to handle the volume, and he would be compelled to bring out his front-end loader, as he had been compelled during the Great

Blizzard that had stranded Laura at the convalescent home.

It was tedious work but he did not mind it, enjoyed it in fact. Save for the purr of the engine, the cushioned scrape of the plow against gravel, and the fitful howl of the wind, the world he moved through was a silent one, all sounds muffled by the blanketing snow. And a pure world, cleansed, white. The vast fields of low-lying cranberry vines, in fair weather an undulating carpet in shades of reds and greens that varied with the seasons, had been transformed into a measureless arctic plane, and the trees of the bordering woods had taken on gothic shapes that…

Whatever metaphor it was for snow-covered trees taking on fanciful shapes that might otherwise have crystallized in Frank's mind was doomed to be stillborn. A snow-covered shape, but this one far from arboreal, caught his attention, shattered his train of thought.

The shape lay to one side of the dirt track, at a point shortly after the track left the clearing and began to snake through the swamp. At first Frank mistook it for a fallen bough half buried in wind-swept snow. But it was too compact for a bough, too human in form. And since when did boughs wear boots?

He stopped the pickup a yard or two short of the object—he hadn't quite convinced himself that it was a man lying there; but what else could it be?—and slid down from the cab. A few paces closer told him it was a man all right; besides the telltale boots there was no mistaking the human contour under the snow, nor the wisp of hair exposed by a sudden gust.

He knelt beside it (already in his mind it was a dead body, not a living man) and prying a wrist free of the snow felt for a pulse.

Nothing.

He couldn't be sure of course, he was no doctor, but the blue of the exposed flesh told its own story. And an ugly gash above the man's left eye that had left on the snow pack beneath it a patch of frozen red slush, like a child's spilled drink, did not inspire hope. Leaving the man he returned to the cab for his phone and punched in 9-1-1.

If he was absolutely sure the man was dead he was not to move the body or otherwise disturb it he was told. If however there was the faintest possibility that the man was still alive Frank should cover him in blankets and keep beside him until help arrived.

Frank was absolutely sure. Besides, he had no blankets with him. If he drove to the house to fetch any, the man, if not frozen now, would be by the time he returned—frozen solid enough to serve as a lawn ornament. His best course was to spread his jacket over the man and wait for the emergency vehicles. And while doing so continue plowing as far as the paved road; otherwise he doubted whether a cruiser or ambulance could make it over the dirt track, with its abrupt twists and turns, so characteristic of old Indian trails, without coming to grief in the drifts.

He was not concerned with obliterating footprints that might provide information as to how the man got to where he was, or how much time had expired since. The falling snow had already accomplished that. Besides, it was obvious that the man had walked in from the road. There was no other way through the dense swamp, even in summer.

But why? Had he become lost? Had he been seeking help, his car having broken down on the road? If so, why hadn't he phoned 9-1-1? Maybe his phone wasn't working. Maybe it needed charging. Or maybe he didn't own one. But if his car had broken down and he was unable to summon help for whatever reason he would have been better off remaining in it until he could flag down a passing vehicle. True, not many vehicles were on the roads in this weather, but the town plows made regular rounds and would have passed by eventually. And what of the gash on his forehead? Had he slipped and struck his head on a rock?

The first cruiser arrived just as Frank, having cleared the dirt track as far as the paved road, was in the process of breaking through the dam blocking the entrance to his drive which the town plow had created when it made its swipe over the pavement and had flung the snow to the side. U-turning, Frank led the cruiser to the spot where the body lay, then drove on to the clearing, where he left the pickup at the edge of the bog before making his way, shivering without his jacket, back on foot.

Frank stood to one side as the responding officers knelt beside the body. The snowfall from the sky had abated somewhat, though not the whirlpools of loose snow churned up by the wind. Jacketless, and blinded by relentless whiplashes Frank sought the refuge of his pickup. As he sat in the cab with the heater cranked up a second cruiser arrived on the scene, followed in rapid succession by a fire rescue team and an ambulance. Blue and red flashing lights bounced off the ubiquitous white in a garish dance macabre, mimicking the flames of Hell, as if hordes of demons had gathered from the nether regions to celebrate the acquisition of another damned soul.

After speaking briefly to one of the officers Frank drove back to the house. There he found his daughters where he had left them, in their rooms, oblivious to the dramatic events of the morning. He chose not to enlighten them; he could do that later, once the body had been removed.

He would, of course, be questioned by the police. He had already made a statement to the responding officer, but he would be asked to give the same information again, perhaps a number of times. If the police found the death at all suspicious, he would be their prime, and perhaps their only, suspect.

The knock at the door came sooner than expected.

When Frank answered it he was confronted by a male officer in mufti.

The man introduced himself. "Mr. Gallerani, I'm Detective Benjamin Andrade. May I come in? I have a few questions."

More than a few, Frank guessed. Nonetheless, the fact that Detective Andrade came alone was a good sign. So far the police were not deeming the death suspicious; otherwise a pair of detectives would have shown up.

He took the man's coat and hat and hung them on a hook.

Wiping his feet on the doormat, Andrade apologized for tracking in snow as he followed Frank into the parlor.

Frank recognized Andrade. He'd seen photos of him displayed in the New Bedford *Standard Times* and other local papers. And he remembered seeing him at town meetings and once or twice shopping at Lloyd's Market. Despite recent growth Rochester was still a small rural community. If everyone didn't know everyone else, they at least knew everyone else's cousin.

Frank offered him a seat by the Franklin stove, close to his own.

"This fire sure feels good," Andrade said. He made a show of rubbing his hands vigorously before the hearth. His fingers were long and tapered, like a concert pianist's, or—at the other end of the spectrum—a safecracker's, and were in keeping with the rest of his physique. Even seated he gave the impression of being tall and lanky—though *lanky* might not be an apt description; *wiry* seemed more apropos. He wore his hair short, even by police standards. He was dark complexioned—of Cape Verdean descent, judging by his Portuguese name.

Leaning forward in his chair he came right to the point: "Mr. Gallerani, can you tell me how you came to discover the body."

Frank obliged him. Having been in law enforcement himself, he knew the drill, and was prepared for a long session.

"Do you have any idea as to what he was doing on your property? Is he anyone you know?"

Frank shook his head. "No to both questions. Of course I didn't get a good look at his face. He was half buried in snow. Once I realized the man was dead I took care not to disturb anything." He shrugged. "Other than to toss my jacket over the body."

Andrade nodded. "Been watching crime shows on TV."

"Actually, I used to be in law enforcement myself. Nothing so dramatic as homicide investigations, but I do understand the importance of not contaminating evidence." He explained to the detective that he had for a number of years worked in New Bedford at the BSI—the Bureau of Special Investigations—for the Welfare Department. "I investigated Welfare fraud for the Commonwealth of Massachusetts."

"Your job involved computers more than field work, I would guess," Andrade said.

"Not really. Computers were an important part of fraud investigation of course, but not so much my bailiwick. I did interviews, stake-outs, even some undercover. I could probably map out from memory every alleyway, underpass, and vacant lot in the city. Not to mention every seedy bar, hole-in-the-wall, and greasy spoon."

"Quite a contrast to this," Andrade observed, with a nod at their surroundings: the cozy room with its warm fire and, outside, the snow-smothered expanse of bog and swamp and woods stretching as far as the eye could see.

"That was the idea," Frank said. He paused. "Can I offer you something? Coffee. Tea. Juice."

"Coffee, if it's not too much trouble. Black."

Frank went into the kitchen, returning minutes later with two steaming mugs.

"Someone's fond of loud music," Andrade remarked with a wry grin.

Frank smiled. "My daughters. Unfortunately they don't care for the same bands, or groups, or whatever they're called these days. They seem to have a running competition as to whose music can drown out the other's. It makes the cacophony of what passes for music these days even worse, if that's possible."

They sat and enjoyed their coffee. Andrade seemed in no hurry to leave—understandable, given the nor'easter raging outside. But Frank guessed he might have another motive for prolonging his stay.

"Have you I.D.'d the body?" Frank asked, when it became apparent that the detective, nursing his second mugful, felt no need to carry on a casual conversation.

"Well, yes, we have," Andrade said, setting the now empty mug on a small drinks table. "Tentatively, of course. That is, assuming the man was carrying his own wallet."

"Is there any reason to believe that he wasn't?" Frank asked.

"Oh no. None at all. I was just being super cautious." He chuckled. "I've taken the witness stand too many times I guess." He nodded his head up and down slowly. "So yes, I think I can safely say we have a positive I.D. The picture on his driver's license matched his face, little cause for doubt there."

"I'm curious," Frank said. "Why would a stranger be walking down my road in this weather? Unless he was someone who got lost. Can you give me his name?"

"No reason not to," Andrade said amiably. "So long as you keep it to yourself until the next of kin are notified." He glanced around the room, as if expecting to see the man's parents hiding in a corner. "His name is Peter Gilbert."

Frank was taken aback. "Peter Gilbert! The landscaper?"

Andrade's almond-shaped eyes narrowed. He looked at Frank with renewed interest. "You know him?"

Frank made a vague gesture with his hands. "Peter did some work for me—let's see, about seven years ago. When we first moved here. My wife wanted the yard spruced up," he added, as if some sort of explanation was needed. In truth he felt stunned, with the sudden knowledge that the body he had discovered in the snow, yet had not recognized, belonged to someone he knew personally. Someone he had known for quite a long time.

"And yet you didn't recognize him."

Frank shook his head. "No. You saw him. He was camou-flaged by a layer of snow. And death alters a man."

"That it does indeed," Andrade agreed. Casually he added: "So you only knew Peter Gilbert professionally? As someone you'd hired as a landscaper?"

Frank chose his next words carefully. "More than profession-ally, I'd say. The fact is, I hired Peter in the first place because I had previously made his acquaintance, and I believed him to be an honest man. Someone who if hired would deliver the goods. And in the end I was right. My wife and I were highly satisfied with the job he did for us. Besides doing the general landscaping he helped me restore an old stone wall that runs alongside the house. If it weren't for a foot of snow on top of it you'd be able to see for yourself," he added lamely.

Andrade touched the tips of the fingers of both hands to-gether, like someone about to pray. "You say you were acquainted with him. How did that come about?"

Frank hesitated. How much should he reveal? What, exactly, did Detective Andrade need to know about Frank's relationship to Peter Gilbert?

"I first became acquainted with Peter in the course of an investigation I was conducting. Medicaid fraud. Peter had nothing to do with it, except that he happened to know one of the principals involved. There was no question of his own involvement. He just happened to be at the wrong place at the wrong time."

That, as Frank well knew, was not strictly true. If there was a Recording Angel somewhere keeping a tally of little white lies, Frank had just earned another tick next to his name.

"In fact, he helped me out of a tight spot." No need to elaborate, unless Andrade pressed him.

Andrade did not press him. Why should he? These were just routine questions.

"And you have no clue as to why, during a bad-ass nor'easter, he would be walking on the drive leading to your house—which, if you'll pardon my English, is located at what some folks might term the asshole of the world."

"No clue whatsoever. As to the location of the house…"

"Nothing personal, Mr. Gallerani. But even by the standards of rural Rochester you have to admit that this is far from—how's that expression go?—far from the maddening crowd."

"Madding crowd," Frank corrected. "*Far from the Madding Crowd*. It's the title of a novel by Thomas Hardy." Rather than taking offense at Andrade's crude description of his chosen isolation, he was only too happy to divert the conversation away from his connection to Peter Gilbert. True, that connection had been innocent enough.

But there were substrata best left buried.

CHAPTER VII

Lena Takes a Licking

Frank swung his truck onto the circular drive and parked behind Lena Lombardi's sedan. The old beat-up Ford pickup she used for odd jobs around her bog was nowhere to be seen. Probably out back somewhere buried deep in snow.

It had been a while since Frank last visited Lena. Not since early fall, shortly before harvest. Since that time little about her place had changed. Like spectators at a bare-knuckle fist fight, clumps of evergreens and deciduous shrubs crowded around the foundation of the two-story house. The shrubs needed pruning. If not for these, the Greek-revival, with its fresh coat of white paint applied the preceding summer, might have blended in with the snow-covered landscape—the cranberry bog and surrounding swamp—rendering it invisible from the road.

He shed his gloves. From the seat beside him he grabbed a bottle of Hob Nob pinot noir by the neck and exited the pickup, slamming the door shut. He stood for a moment *en plein air* before moving on to the house. After the closeness of the cab the crisp cold air tasted good, like chilled vodka on a parched throat. As he made his way across the ice-slick drive his frosted breath, a wispy emanation of the life force within him, curled skyward, like chimney smoke, but dissipated just inches away, as if symbolic of the transitory nature of human existence.

Peter Gilbert's death had left him shaken.

He paused again to glance at the blue expanse above him. Nary a cloud in sight. It would be nice if the weather stayed this way until spring. Like most New Englanders, although Frank took pleasure in all four seasons, winter was his least favorite; by mid-February he was heartily sick of snow and ice and freezing temperatures, eager to see grasses and sedges sprouting forth from the sodden ground, trees leafing out, the chameleon-like metamorphosing of carpeted cranberry bogs from maroon to soft green as tiny buds formed on the vines.

He took long, deep breaths of the tonic air, then mounted the steps to the wood-columned portico, with its ornate eaves and door surrounds, and wiped as best he could the snow from the soles of his boots onto the welcome-mat. Shifting the Hob Nob to his left hand, he rapped loudly on the door with the knuckles of his right.

After a minute or so, having received no response, he rapped again.

This time there was no delay. The door opened immediately.

Now, there was no denying it, the face that confronted Frank belonged to his dear friend Lena Lombardi. But it was a contorted version of that face, its nose wrinkled, its brows askew, its features all twisted awry, as if her head was made of putty which some prankish child had gotten hold of, and was busily distorting for the amusement of his friends. Alternatively, she looked like a victim of the Inquisition after the pious torturers had spent an hour or two attempting to persuade her of the error of her ways.

As Frank gaped open-mouthed at the spectacle, the septuagenarian brought a paper towel close to her mouth, into which she gagged repeatedly.

Her gagging brought to mind a time many years ago when Frank, investigating a case of Food Stamp Fraud in New Bedford, had come upon a maggot-ridden corpse in a basement apartment. The putrid cadaver was that of a corpulent man who had been dead for at least a month—from mid July to mid August. Judging by the swarms of bloated flies crowding the corpse, several generations had gorged and gone forth to multiply on the putrescent bounty.

Frank's immediate reaction to the stench in that charnel house, though different from that of the feasting flies, bore much in common with Lena's current convulsions.

Alarmed, he slipped by her into the living room, pulling the door shut behind him. "Lena! What's wrong?"

His question drew no response, save for further gagging.

"Are you ill?"

She shook her head. "I'm…fine," she gasped. Holding up her hand with a motion to indicate that she would return shortly, she dashed off toward the kitchen.

Frank followed at a more sedate pace. When he arrived in the kitchen he could hear her in the bathroom. Judging from the sounds that issued forth she was, of all things, brushing her teeth.

Had she gone mad? Ever since he'd known her she'd always been somewhat eccentric—but this was to the extreme.

Something rubbed against his pants leg.

"Marmalade! What's wrong with your mistress? Has she finally gone off the deep end?"

"I heard that!" Lena shouted from behind the bathroom door.

Frank stooped down to pet the cat. From the bathroom came sounds of gargling.

Purring, Marmalade rolled over on his back so that Frank could scratch his belly.

"He doesn't let just anyone do that," Lena remarked as she emerged from the bathroom. "It must be because he knows you're family."

In reality, although they called each other "cousin," Frank and Lena were not related by blood. Frank's father, deceased, was Lena's late husband's cousin. But the two, although they had known each other only a few years, were fast friends.

"So what was the impersonation of a gargoyle all about?" Frank asked as he straightened to a standing position. "Was the sight of me standing at the door that upsetting?"

Lena ignored the witticism. An eye to the Hob Nob, she responded with a question of her own: "Here or in the library?"

"The library, I think," Frank replied. "The kitchen smells of fish."

"Marmalade's dinner."

While Frank opened the wine Lena fetched two stem glasses from a cupboard and preceded him into the library, where they made themselves comfortable. Only after the wine had been poured did Lena offer an explanation.

"Gargoyle impersonation. Not very flattering, but I suppose apropos."

"I wish I had it on video. On the Internet it would go viral."

"I'm not hooked to the Internet, so I wouldn't know," Lena countered, with an exaggerated frown. She was, however, capable of laughing at herself, and did so. "I'd settle for an old-fashioned snapshot," she added after a pause.

"I'll settle for an explanation," Frank said. "How do you like this pinot noir?"

"It's excellent. In fact, just what the doctored ordered, after my, uh, contretemps."

"Which was…?"

Lena sighed. "I was in the kitchen, making a mock cherry pie from cranberries I froze last fall."

"Mock cherry pie. My favorite."

"It's a very old recipe," Lena said. "My mother's mother

handed it down to her."

"And after obtaining if from you I've handed it over to Laura," Frank said with a grin.

"When does your poor wife have time to cook?"

"She doesn't. Which is why I visit you whenever I can." He sipped his pinot noir. "Lena, you're stalling."

"Okay, I'll get on with it," she said. "You have to realize, though, that if you hadn't caught me *in flagrante delicto*, as it were, I would have taken my secret with me to the grave. Anyhow, I had cooked up the filling—cranberries, raisins, sugar, salt, flour—in a saucepan on the stove and set it aside to cool. Beside it I placed the spoon I'd stirred it with. I would have licked the spoon—I always lick spoons and bowls whenever I'm finishing up part of a recipe, to make sure I've gotten it just right—but Marmalade was making such a pest of himself, weaving in and out between my ankles, that it was either feed him then and there or risk tripping over him and breaking my neck."

Perhaps because he heard his name, or perhaps because he merely sought company, the orange tabby chose that moment to saunter into the room. His limp, souvenir of the time several years ago when he had been deliberately shot, and nearly died, was hardly noticeable. Despite her pique with the cat Lena could not refrain from casting an affectionate glance his way.

"As you know, he's inordinately fond of seafood, the smellier the better—you caught a whiff of it in the kitchen—so I opened a can and spooned it into his dish. I set the empty can with the spoon in it on the counter to rinse out later and got on with my cooking."

"I think I know what's coming," Frank said. "More wine?" Without waiting for an answer—inevitably it would be yes—he refilled her glass.

"I was chopping up vegetables for tonight's supper, when I

remembered that I still had the spoon with the cranberry filling to lick. Just then I heard your knock on the door..."

"And, distracted, picked up the wrong spoon: the one steeped in cat food instead of the one coated with the cranberry filling," Frank finished for her. "Tell me, Lena, had you downed a few sherries beforehand?"

"Certainly not!" Lena said, indignant. Then, with a Cheshire grin: "It was port, I had only one glass, and it had nothing to do with the incident."

"The best chefs sip wine while they're cooking," Frank observed. "Or so I'm told." He chuckled. "So my arrival was opportune. It enabled me to see Lena Lombardi's famous Lon Chaney impersonation."

"Enough small talk, Frank," Lena said abruptly, but not without an inward laugh at her own expense. "I want to hear your story while there's still some pinot noir left in my glass."

The day he discovered the corpse—Peter Gilbert's body—on his property Frank had immediately phoned Lena, before she had a chance to hear about it from the news media. To have done otherwise would have been to incur her displeasure. Naturally, he was reluctant to discuss the details over the phone; for her part, Lena preferred a face-to-face telling, at which she could freely interrogate the witness and interject her own observations at will—while at the same time partaking of a glass or two of the fermented juice of the grape.

Three days had elapsed since the nor'easter and the Grim Reaper's unexpected house call. During that time Lena had waited patiently, knowing that her reward for forbearance would be the additional information Frank was sure to glean from the police in the meantime. Her interest in the matter was, of course, entirely altruistic. She fancied herself an amateur detective; as such, she was eager to offer her services to the police in solving the case in the event that criminal activity was involved—whether the police wanted her assistance or not.

Frank for his part was fully aware of his friend's proclivities. His motives, however, in acceding to her request for, as she put it, an "intimate tête-à-tête" were not entirely disinterested. Sure, he wanted to humor her, to provide her with an insider's account of his discovery of the body and subsequent events in order to gratify her curiosity. But he also, despite her eccentricity, valued her intuitive insight, and would be appreciative of any advice—or assistance—she might offer.

"Now Frank, be sure to start at the beginning. I want to hear each and every detail, no matter how seemingly insignificant."

"The beginning? No. I'll start with the storm, then the body, and work backwards. You'll understand why once I've explained."

"So you knew this Peter Gilbert," Lena said when he'd finished the first part of his story. "Even though at first you didn't recognize him." She paused, weighing her words. "I have a gut feeling that you didn't tell Detective Andrade the whole truth."

"Your gut is right on target," Frank admitted. Idly, he drummed his fingers on the table next to him, and eyed his empty glass.

"I could open a bottle of Meiomi," Lena suggested. "That is, if you'll stay for supper. I wouldn't want you to drive home impaired."

Frank shook his head. "I don't want to leave the girls alone. The bus drops them off at a friend's house, and I pick them up around four. Their friend's mother won't mind if I'm a half hour or so late, but I don't like to impose. She's driven them home a few times, when for whatever reason I couldn't pick them up. But like I said, I don't like leaving them alone. Especially after…"

Lena leaned forward. "The real story, Frank."

"I've never told this to anyone," Frank said. "Not even to Laura. It happened—oh, it must be close to twenty years ago…"

CHAPTER VIII

Rat's Requiem

Jack Bartlett had reminded Frank of something he'd once seen crawl out of a rotting carcass by the side of the road.

Sitting across from Lena, sipping wine in her library, Frank conjured up in his mind that day in his office, the phone letting off a loud raspberry just as the weasel-face Bartlett was about to mouth another lie.

"Bureau of Special Investigations." Frank said. He listened to the voice coming in over the line but kept his gaze focused on his reluctant guest.

Bartlett sank back into the visitor's chair, letting his eyes dart about the room as if seeking a means of escape, or more likely, objects of value which he might easily slip into his pocket.

The voice on the line belonged to Laura Silva, Frank's fiancée. Frank—finding repugnant the idea of chatting to the woman he loved in the presence of Jack "The Rat" Bartlett—cut the conversation short. He'd explain to her later.

Jack "The Rat" Bartlett was a convicted child molester whose victims of choice had been toddlers. Unfortunately Bartlett's sordid past was irrelevant to Frank's investigation of Welfare fraud.

"You're too stupid to run a Food Stamp scam of this magnitude on your own. Tell me who your bosses are and I'll put in a word with the DA. Otherwise…"

"Otherwise kiss my ass." Bartlett hissed the words out through rotten teeth, then followed the hiss with a gurgling sound, as if choking on his own vomit.

"Suit yourself. You know what they do to your kind in prison."

"You ain't got nothing on me. I'm clean."

"Yeah, like an open sewer in Calcutta." He rose from the desk. "I'm through wasting my time. Run along now. Go home and brush your teeth. What's left of them."

Living up to his sobriquet, Jack "The Rat" Bartlett quickly sprang from his seat and scurried out through the door. To cleanse the air Frank crossed the room and cracked open a window. He stood before it, looking down. His second-story suite commanded a panoramic view of the New Bedford Welfare Office parking lot.

Bartlett emerged from the building and threaded his way through the lines of cars, glancing furtively left and right as if fearful of pursuit. He climbed behind the wheel of a maroon late model Buick—Food Stamp fraud evidently paid well these days—and sped away south on Acushnet Avenue.

Frank returned to his desk. One niggling task remained before he could call it a day.

He perused a ream of dot matrix printouts. A cursory reading seemed to bear out his suspicions that a local pharmacy was bilking Medicaid by dispensing generic drugs while billing for higher-priced brand names.

He shoved the printouts to a corner of the desk and glanced at his watch. Just short of five thirty. Time enough to swing by the South End before heading over to Laura's apartment.

The pharmacy occupied a corner of a rehabbed brick warehouse. Frank parked in front of a Portuguese bar and grille. Hand-lettered signs taped to the restaurant's windows advertised *vinho verde*, stuffed quahogs and cacoila sandwiches. The rich aroma of fried linguica and chourico wafted into the warm September evening. What would Laura be serving for supper? Something Portuguese, he hoped.

A half dozen store fronts between the restaurant and pharmacy were boarded up. A three-decker across the street showed evidence of a recent fire. Children playing shouted to one another in a melange of English, Portuguese, and Spanish.

Frank pushed through the pharmacy doors. He paused at the magazine rack and, while pretending to leaf through the tabloids, kept an eye on the pharmacist, who was busy behind the counter.

Her name tag read *Beatrice Souza*. Dark complexioned, in her mid twenties—fresh out of graduate school he guessed—she was pretty in a chunky sort of way. She waited on a teenaged mother with a sick child in tow, then occupied herself counting pills into bottles.

A man entered the store and made his way directly to the dispensing area. Beatrice gripped the counter as if to defend herself. The man appeared to be in his early thirties. Heavy set, six feet four or taller, he lumbered down the aisle like a Mack truck in climbing gear. Before he could speak Beatrice said something in a low voice which seemed to anger him.

As the two argued Frank could make out only bits and pieces: the man, whose name was Pete, was upset by something Beatrice had done or intended to do. Something about smuggling illegal aliens?

An elderly woman clutching a prescription slip shuffled up to the counter. Beatrice seized the opportunity and broke off her conversation. Pete hesitated, then swung on his heels and stomped out of the store.

Frank continued to browse, eventually selecting a copy of *New Bedford Magazine*, which he paid for as he left.

Dusk had sifted onto the street, accentuating the shadows, sending the children home to supper and TV. As he headed toward his car Frank spotted Bartlett's Buick parked across the street, and Jack "The Rat" himself ducking into an alley that cut along the side of the old warehouse.

When Frank stepped into Laura's apartment the exquisite aroma of kale soup informed him that his wish for a Portuguese repast was about to be fulfilled. On the dining room table a stack of freshly baked rolls stood within easy reach. He grabbed Laura—and a roll.

"Watch those Italian hands." She received his kiss while gently prying his fingers from her buttocks.

"Man cannot live by Portuguese rolls alone."

"How about kale soup? Plus a glass or two of *vinho verde*. And an occasional kiss."

They had been dating now for several months. Frank was beginning to believe Laura really meant it when she said, "Not until we're married."

He helped her set the table. When they had settled down to eat he said, "Sorry I was brusque when you called," and explained his feelings about Jack "The Rat" Bartlett. "It's as though he pollutes the very air around him."

"He doesn't sound like someone I'd like to meet in a dark alley."

"Funny you should say that. That's precisely where I last saw him—entering a dark alley." He told her of his visit to the pharmacy.

"Is there a connection between this character's involvement with Food Stamp fraud and the drug store's rip off of Medicaid?"

"None that I can figure out. Bartlett buys coupons from junkies and winos at twenty-five cents the dollar, then passes them on for fifty cents. Penny ante stuff. Whereas the pharmacy bills for brand names while dispensing generics. At a cost to Joe Taxpayer of tens of thousands a year."

Laura ladled soup into Frank's nearly empty plate and poured herself a second glass of wine. "Coincidence?"

"What was he doing in the alley?"

"He's a child molester. Do you suppose . . .?"

"He's holding a child prisoner? Bartlett's not that stupid. At least I hope he isn't."

He turned his attention to the kale soup. Laura made it the way he liked—thick with potatoes and chunks of linguica. As he sopped his plate clean with a torn Portuguese roll he mused aloud. "He wouldn't park on the street in plain view. He's too devious for that. Besides, with his contacts he can rent a child. No need to kidnap."

Laura dropped her spoon into her plate. "I think I'm losing my appetite."

He reached over and patted her hand. "Sorry." He poured them each another glass of *vinho verde*.

"Trying to ply me with drink, huh? I'm wise to your profligate ways."

He left Laura's shortly before eleven and took a detour through the South End. Despite a CLOSED sign on the door, lights blazed in the pharmacy. He could discern Beatrice Souza and a female cashier moving about. Bartlett's Buick was still there—but on the opposite side of the street.

Frank swung to the curb near a darkened house. He angled the rear view mirror so that he could take in both the pharmacy and the entrance to the alley. After a while the cashier exited through the front door and drove off in a beige Toyota. Beatrice remained inside.

He crossed the street and glanced into the window. Beatrice sat hunched at the far end of the store before a computer terminal. Dedicated employee? Or scam artist doctoring the day's transactions?

The alley, situated between the pharmacy and a vacant building, lay steeped in shadows. He slipped into the entrance and felt his way along the wall. Light splashing from the headlamps of a passing car revealed a dumpster, and beyond it, the pharmacy's rear fire exit.

As Frank groped through the darkness his foot struck a hard object and he lost his balance. Lurching forward, he sent the object—an empty beer bottle—skittering over the asphalt.

In the stillness that ensued he heard a faint rustling. He crouched behind the dumpster.

Beyond the fire exit, in a section of the building that appeared to be a vacant warehouse, a door swung ajar. As light spilled into the alley Jack "The Rat" poked his head into the night air and inched forward, keeping his hand against the jamb. Satisfied, apparently, that all was well he stepped back, drawing the door after him.

Before he could shut it tight a form emerged from the shadows and seizing the knob yanked the door open. Caught off guard Bartlett tumbled into the alley.

The form—whom Frank recognized as Pete, the man he'd seen arguing with Beatrice Souza—grabbed Bartlett by the scruff of the neck and shook him like a mastiff worrying a rat.

"Piece of shit!" In his fury Pete backed into the edge of the door, tripped, and loosened his grip. Breaking free, Bartlett scooted from the alley into the street. With a curse Pete lumbered after him.

Frank flattened himself against the wall. He waited a moment then followed as far as the mouth of the alley—in time to see Bartlett hunched at the wheel of the Buick and Pete grabbing for the door handle. The engine coughed into life and Jack "The Rat" sped off, leaving Pete with a fistful of empty air.

A grating sound issued from the alley. Frank hugged the shadows as the warehouse door gaped like an open wound. An Asian male in his late teens appeared in the doorway, clutched the knob and pulled the door shut.

A car cruised by, rap music booming from its open windows.

Through the plate glass window Frank saw Beatrice standing with her arms folded and Pete gesticulating wildly. If Beatrice was afraid of Pete she gave no sign of it. She held her ground while he vented his anger. With a contemptuous laugh she said something that must have hit its mark. Tossing up his hands in disgust he stomped out.

Crossing the street, he climbed into the cab of a green pickup. If Frank expected a theatrical exit replete with grinding gears he was disappointed. Easing the pickup away from the curb Pete drove off at a moderate speed.

The lettering on the door read *Peter Gilbert, Landscaping*.

Leaving Beatrice to her midnight lucubrations, Frank drove home.

He spent the following morning sifting through computer documents.

After a late lunch at a local Portuguese hole-in-the-wall (they made a hell of a codfish Gomes de Sa) he returned to the Welfare Office and flipped through the Yellow Pages, where he found an ad for *Peter Gilbert, Landscaping* and an Acushnet address.

Crossing the hallway to the Child Support Enforcement Unit, he tiptoed over to a computer terminal where a heavyset woman sat pounding the keys. He tapped her on the shoulder.

"That you, handsome?"

He leaned over and kissed her cheek.

Susan Goodwin glanced up from the computer with a grin. Twice Frank's age, and a grandmother several times over, she never missed an opportunity to flirt.

"You're in a good mood. Laura treating you well? Or—let me guess. I've got it! You want something. Certainly not my body. An address maybe?"

"It's your body I really want. But I'll settle for a Social Security number."

"Anything for a friend. And I do mean anything."

Five minutes later Susan popped into his office waving a computer printout.

"You're working for the wrong department, Susie. You should leave Child Support and come over to BSI."

"And make Laura jealous? My conscience wouldn't allow."

Armed with Peter Gilbert's Social Security number Frank set to work. An hour later, bleary-eyed, he flicked off the monitor to his computer and stretched his legs. Peter Gilbert was clean. He paid his taxes, obeyed the traffic laws. If he had an arrest record it was under a different name, a different number.

What now?

Go home and get a good night's sleep. Let the folks in Boston deal with Beatrice Souza and the peccant pharmacy. As for Jack "The Rat" Bartlett—Frank had enough hard evidence for a conviction for Food Stamp fraud.

Yeah. A meaningless fine, a few months in jail. And Jack "The Rat," predator, back on the streets. Frank recalled a four-year-old girl with gonorrhea. Bartlett had got away scot free on that one.

He ate supper at Muldoon's Saloon—a stuffed quahog followed by French meat pie—then drove to the pharmacy, parking in the same spot as the previous night. Fifteen minutes later Bartlett pulled up to the curb, bundled out of the Buick, and scuttled across the street into the alley. Three or four plastic grocery bags swung from his hands like loose luggage. Moments later he reappeared sans bags.

When the Buick pulled from the curb Frank swung after it, keeping several lengths behind. Bartlett drove like a man without a care in the world, obeying all stop signs and red lights, yielding to pedestrians. Nearing the waterfront, where traffic thinned, he increased his speed but kept well within the limit.

After a score or more of seemingly meaningless turns the Buick came to an unexpected halt on a darkened pier. Caught off guard, Frank drove by, pretending to be lost, hoping he hadn't been recognized.

Backtracking a block or two, he found a cul-de-sac between a seafood wholesaler and a fishermen's union hall, both closed for the night. Grabbing a flashlight, he left his car and proceeded on foot.

Though ill-lit, the piers were not entirely deserted. Occasionally a vehicle passed. Once, he imagined he spotted Peter Gilbert's pickup but dismissed the notion as an illusion brought about by nerves and the dazzle of head lights.

Bartlett's Buick was not alone. A half dozen vehicles dotted the asphalt lot—belonging in all likelihood to the crews of the various trawlers tied at the dock. From two of the vessels lights shone like lanterns at an outdoor party. From a radio tuned to a Portuguese station the plaintive sounds of *fado*—songs of love and fate—drifting across the water broke the nocturnal silence. An odor, raw and pungent, redolent of dead creatures from the sea and ocean-churning engines, permeated the September evening.

The glow from the fishing boats seemed to intensify the gloom. With his flashlight switched off Frank approached the Buick. It was empty.

He crossed to the center of the pier, casually, like a wharfinger out for a stroll. The radio announcer barked something in Portuguese. Frank heard what sounded like a groan.

It was followed by another. Louder. Switching on the flashlight he played the beam up and down the pier and immediately located the source: Bartlett, lying on the asphalt in a rumpled heap, next to a caboose-like storage shed. His fingers clawed at the shed as if he was trying to pull himself upright.

Frank hurried to the prostrate form. Bartlett's eyes were half-open, his breathing irregular. Frank knelt to assist him. Hearing a scuffling sound he glanced up, too late, as two men leapt from behind the shed.

The men jerked him to his feet and pinned his arms behind his back. The flashlight clattered against the pavement.

Bartlett scrambled to his feet, scooped up the flashlight and with a leer shoved it in Frank's face.

"Sucker."

Frank struggled to free himself but the men tightened their grip. The stench of dead fish and cheap booze betrayed them: lumpers out for an easy buck. Off-loading trawlers or stoving in skulls, it was all in a day's work.

"You been following me. How come?"

"To remind you to brush your teeth."

Bartlett kneed him in the groin.

Frank sagged forward, nausea rippling through his gut like an after shock. Far away, the radio's disembodied voice sang *fado*, a lament for lost love.

"Use the ice pick, Rat," one of the lumpers suggested.

"In there." Bartlett nodded toward the shed. To Frank he said: "I'm gonna start with your eyes."

As the lumpers hustled Frank into the shed they adjusted their grip. He twisted to one side and, freeing an arm, jabbed his elbow into the midriff of the lumper who had suggested the ice pick. With an *ooph* of expelled air the man doubled over. Frank pirouetted and slammed his fist into the face of the second man.

Bartlett swung the flashlight hard against Frank's skull. As Frank staggered against the shed door it swung inward. He steadied himself as his assailants closed in. He groped in the shed for a weapon—an ax, a gaff, a length of pipe. Anything.

Above the radio's drone he heard the thud of feet against pavement.

Wielding a tire iron, Peter Gilbert arrived on the scene and set upon the two lumpers, fetching the first a blow upon the shoulder, the second a jab to the kneecap. The sound of bones cracking was music to Frank's ears.

Seeing the lumpers crumple like smashed toys Bartlett turned tail and scooted to the end of the pier. Frank followed, and grabbing a handful of jacket swung "The Rat" around. Momentum wrested the jacket from Frank's grasp and Bartlett pitched over the side, bouncing off a piling and hitting the water with a splash.

Frank leaned over. Bartlett flailed his arms wildly, frantic to keep his head above water. Frank reached down, hesitated, then slowly withdrew his hand as Jack "The Rat" Bartlett, blowing bubbles, sank deep below the surface.

CHAPTER IX

The Thought Plickens

"You could have saved him," Lena said.

"Yes."

"But instead you let him drown."

"Yes."

Lena cast a rueful eye at her empty wineglass. "It's what I would have done," she said at last. "The rat. I would have watched him sink, ever so slowly, and if his eyelids happened to flutter upward as he turned purple from sucking in water, I would have smiled and waved goodbye with my fingers. You know, the way you wave to a toddler: 'Tootle-oo, sweetheart.'"

They sat in silence for a while.

"I'll probably never get to finishing baking that pie," Lena said finally.

"I'm keeping you," Frank said, though he made no move to get up from his chair.

"Not at all. I was only making the pie for something to do. The filling will keep. Truth be told, I'd rather ponder mysteries any day." She glanced at their empty wineglasses. "Can I offer you coffee, and perhaps a cranberry muffin?"

Frank shook his head. "No, thanks."

"What time do you have to shove off?"

"Soon."

"Have you heard from this Detective…what's his name?"

"Andrade. Benjamin Andrade. He stopped by this morning, after phoning first to make sure I'd be home."

"And…?"

"The plot thickens, as they say." Frank glanced at his watch. "I think I'll have that muffin after all. And coffee, if it's no bother."

"I could use a cup myself," Lena said, and rose from her chair.

Ten minutes later Frank sat holding a cranberry muffin on a paper plate in one hand, a cup of coffee in the other. Marmalade lay sprawled at his feet, ostensibly asleep, though an occasional twitch of his ear signified some degree of alertness.

Frank set the coffee onto his drinks table and tackled the muffin.

"So the thought plickens, heh?" Lena remarked, the spoonerism deliberate. "How so?"

Frank dabbed crumbs from his lips with a paper napkin. "Detective Andrade is becoming quite chummy. Insists that I call him Ben."

"To get you to lower your guard?"

Frank nodded. "I'm glad that you see things my way. I was beginning to wonder whether I might be paranoid."

Lena shook her head knowingly. "Man found dead on your property in unusual circumstances. You report finding the corpse. The wound to his head is recent. You have no explanation as to why this man, Peter Gilbert (of whom you admit having prior knowledge), would be walking down the long, isolated road leading to your house in a near blizzard. Naturally the police are suspicious." She took a meditative sip of her coffee. "There must be something else, though."

"They found his pickup about a mile down the road from the turn into my property. It had skidded off the pavement into the swamp. The strange thing is, his cell phone was in the glove compartment, in perfect working order. He could have called for help, AAA or whatever. But chose not to."

"Had he been drinking I wonder?"

Frank shook his head. "I asked 'Ben' that. It seems an autopsy was performed in New Bedford. No traces of alcohol or drugs. Detective Andrade—somehow I prefer that to Ben—was so kind as to give me a detailed account of the contents of Peter's stomach. It seems he had breakfasted well: coffee; orange juice; an onion, mushroom, and cheddar cheese omelet; whole grain toast."

"What? No bacon?"

"I forgot to mention bacon. That too."

"'The condemned man ate a hearty meal.'" She thought awhile. "Family?"

"Sort of. Peter wasn't married, but he lived with his girlfriend. In Mattapoisett."

"And she can give no explanation as to why he might have been where he was?"

Frank shrugged. "Though he didn't say it outright, Detective Andrade intimated as much."

"Cause of death?"

"Andrade was less forthcoming on that one. My guess is that Peter slipped and fell, hit his head, and froze to death. He wasn't dressed for a nor'easter. Just a sweater and light jacket. These days most people drive around in their shirtsleeves, no matter what the temperature is outside. It doesn't seem to occur to them that their vehicle might break down. Besides, they have cell phones."

"And yet Peter Gilbert didn't use his. Why?"

"Why indeed," Frank said. He glanced at his watch. "It's time I got going."

"Before you go…I'm curious. What do you plan to do, if anything?"

"What can I do? Right now I'm apparently under a cloud, at

least as far as Andrade is concerned. But eventually he'll just have to accept Peter's death as an unexplained mystery."

"With these things you never know though, do you? It would be nice to dispel that cloud."

"Nice, but I don't see how."

"You could visit the girlfriend. Maybe she has knowledge she isn't willing to share with the police."

Frank made a sound that was something akin to a grunt. "Visiting Peter's girlfriend could prove very awkward."

If Lena were a cat, her ears would have at that moment pricked up. "How so?"

"His girlfriend's name is Beatrice Souza."

"Beatrice Sou…Oh! the pharmacist you investigated for fraud twenty years ago."

Frank nodded.

"How did that turn out by the way?"

"Actually, better for her than it should have. Because of Peter—after all, he saved me from a nasty situation—I went as easy on her as I could. In fact I suppressed some of the evidence I had against her, on her promise that she'd go straight."

It was Lena's turn to make a sound: half cough, half grunt.

Frank shrugged. "Yeah, I know. But I felt it was the right thing to do. Anyhow, no jail time. Just probation. But no more practicing as a pharmacist. Not in Massachusetts, anyhow."

"What does she do now?" Lena asked. "Smuggle illegal aliens into the country?"

Frank smiled. "You judge your fellow human beings too harshly, Lena. Last I knew she and Peter had some sort of nursery or greenhouse operation. They bought a piece of land cheap at auction, where an old farmhouse used to be, before the town seized it for back taxes. The old Hickman place I think it was; I remember the name because it was in the local newspaper at the

65

time. The preservationists were in an uproar over the fire department deliberately burning down an antique house, for training purposes, that had been in the same family ever since the early seventeen hundreds. The two bought the land shortly before Peter did the landscaping for me. Far as I know, he kept up the landscaping end of the business, while she ran the nursery."

"It seems to me, Frank, that Beatrice owes you a favor. But if you don't feel comfortable dropping in on her in her time of bereavement, why not attend Peter's funeral? Or at least his wake. That way you could reintroduce yourself."

Frank rose to leave. Bending down to give Marmalade a parting tickle, he said: "I intend to pay my respects at the funeral home, as soon as the police free the body up and visiting hours are established." As he straightened he gave Lena a knowing look. "It will be interesting to see if Detective Andrade makes an appearance."

After her friend had driven away, Lena returned to the kitchen to finish baking her mock cherry pie. Ever hopeful for a morsel, a tidbit, a neglected crumb, whatever the gods of feline beneficence might send his way, Marmalade, tail erect, sauntered in her wake, to make a general pest of himself until, having extorted a sliver of smoked gouda, he sought out his favorite corner for his customary nap.

The pie filling was in the saucepan on the stove where Lena had left it to cool, congealed to the consistency of chewed gum but salvageable. The spoon she had used to stir the filling while it was cooking rested on the counter; the cat-food tainted spoon lay in the sink where she had flung it in disgust.

While the pie was baking in the oven Lena washed the soiled

dishes and put them away. She glanced at the clock on the wall: too early to begin supper. She sat at the kitchen table and gazed out the window, at her Currier and Ives surroundings. Flooded for the winter, the cranberry bog lay beneath a thick sheet of ice. But there were no skaters, as otherwise there might be on a sunny afternoon like this, because deep snow buried the ice, too deep for even the die-hard neighborhood hockey players to scrape away for a makeshift rink.

It had been several years now since she turned over the day-to-day operation of the bog to a cranberry growers' service. After her beloved husband, Rinaldo—Rhino to his friends—still in his thirties, died suddenly of a heart attack and left her a childless widow, she had looked to the formidable tasks raising a cranberry crop entailed as a way to help fill the terrible void she felt at his passing.

Now that she paid others to do the work for her the bog no longer demanded huge chunks of her time, and she was free to seek out more pleasurable pursuits, such as the solving of mysteries—*vide* the puzzler which Frank had (like Marmalade, the carcass of a recently deceased rodent clenched tight in his mouth) just laid at her doorstep.

CHAPTER X

Secret, or Hoax?

Cheryl Fernandes sat before the fireplace in the library in her leather recliner (a gift from Anthony this past Christmas), with her feet resting, and Marmalade dozing on her lap.

"The fire could use another log," she observed.

"Let me get it," Lena said.

As a rule Cheryl, by far the younger of the two, would be the one to rise from her chair to add wood to the fire. Doing so on this occasion, however, would be to incommode Marmalade, whose status in the household lay somewhere between that of pampered child and reigning monarch.

Lena got up from the overstuffed armchair in which she had been cozily ensconced to select several slabs of split maple from the wood stack. After tossing the slabs one by one into the fireplace she raked glowing embers around them, so that within a minute or two the flames were once again roaring cheerily.

"I agree with you, it's a puzzler," Cheryl said, returning to the subject of the evening's conversation. "But I don't see how even you can successfully stick your nose into this one," she added, not without a twinkle in her eye, alluding to her friend's proclivity for snooping.

"You know dear, I'm almost inclined to agree with you," Lena said. "Except that there has to be an explanation, and I'm determined to get at it. Besides, I owe it to Frank."

Cheryl had returned home from her job teaching English Literature at Bridgewater State University later than usual; Lena waited until the younger woman had changed into comfortable clothes and enjoyed the supper she had prepared for them before launching into her (somewhat bowdlerized) recital of Frank's story (leaving out the parts about Frank's deliberate failure to save Jack "The Rat" Bartlett from drowning and his suppression of certain evidence in the Medicaid fraud case against Peter Gilbert's girlfriend, Beatrice Souza).

"You've got nothing to go on," Cheryl insisted.

"There's always the possibility that Frank will unearth something. Some clue as to what this Peter Gilbert was doing walking down a lonely country dirt road during a raging snow storm. The girlfriend—Beatrice Souza—may know more than she's letting on. If Frank gets nowhere maybe I can worm something out of her."

"You can't just show up at her doorstep and start asking questions," Cheryl pointed out.

"No, but I can visit her place of business and shop around. She and Peter bought the old Hickman property and turned it into a nursery. It'll be spring soon. I can always find room around here for another shrub or two."

"Hickman—why does that name ring a bell?"

Cheryl must have twitched, or otherwise shifted her body; for with a slight dig of his claws to express annoyance, Marmalade leapt from her lap to seek out a less mobile cushion on which to snooze.

"It was in the news a few years back, dear. Seven or eight years ago, according to Frank. Although come to think of it, that was before you returned to Massachusetts from North Carolina; you couldn't have heard about it then. Anyhow, the fire department burned the centuries-old farmhouse down as a practice exercise. That made a lot of people unhappy."

"Ah, yes, the Hickman farm," Cheryl said, nodding her head. "Now I remember."

"But you can't dear. Like I said, it was…"

"Not whatever was in the news," Cheryl interrupted. "I'm not talking about that. Something else entirely." She glanced at Lena. "Is it too late for a glass of wine, do you think?"

"Why no, dear," Lena said, taken aback by this unexpected stroke of good fortune, this manna from the skies. "A little nightcap might do us both some good. You've had a grueling day, and I'm always in the mood for wine. That bottle of Meiomi pinot noir we've been saving?" she suggested, sensing that Cheryl had something out of the ordinary to impart.

"Let me get it," Cheryl said, rising from the recliner. "But first, another log on the fire."

Not until they were both once again comfortably seated in front of the cozy fire, and in possession of a glass of pinot noir, did Cheryl explain.

"Last year during spring break, when I was at the school library doing some research for that book of local folklore I've been working on, I came across something quite peculiar."

"Peculiar? Something to do with the Hickman homestead?"

"Uh-huh. In fact, rather than tell you, let me show you. Give me a few minutes to dig through my papers," Cheryl said as she got up to leave the room.

Five minutes later she returned from upstairs with a manila folder, from which she removed a sheaf of papers. "Here, take a look at this." She handed four of the sheets to Lena. "It's probably nothing I can use for my book, but I held on to it anyhow because of its uniqueness. It's all on flash drive, but I like to keep hard copies as a backup."

Lena examined the sheets. They were standard size, eight-and-one-half by eleven inches. They had writing on them, in longhand, presumably in pencil, though she could not tell for sure because these were photocopies, or scans. (Lena knew next to nothing about computers, except what little she gleaned from conversations with Cheryl.)

"Before you read that, let me tell you where I found it," Cheryl said. She paused to take a sip of wine, perhaps to lubricate her vocal cords, or more likely, to prolong Lena's agony of suspense.

"As I said," she continued at last, "I was in the library at Bridgewater State digging around for leads for my book on folklore—when I came across a book titled *Haunted New England: A Devilish View of the Yankee Past*. The book was published in 1972 I believe, though the text itself—fascinating though it is, with true tales of hauntings, pirates, witches, and other weird phenomena—doesn't have anything to do with what you have in your hand. The person who wrote what you're holding wrote it, in longhand as you can see, on the inside of the book's covers and on the flyleaf. I had no problem scanning the material. The book has a lot of photographs, hence the large format."

"Hence," Lena echoed, teasing her college professor friend.

Ignoring the dig, Cheryl went on: "The handwriting is fairly neat; you shouldn't have any difficulty reading it."

Forgetting, for once, the glass of wine at her elbow, Lena took up the first sheet, on the upper left-hand corner of which Cheryl (presumably) had inked in the numeral 1, and began to read:

Yesterday morning I stood concealed behind a tree and watched as the old Hickman farmhouse, reputed to be haunted, burned to the ground.

No, I am not an arsonist. It was not I, but the fire department itself that set fire to the historic building, as a way both to test equipment and to train new firefighters. The event—perhaps because of the controversy surrounding it—was not open to the public. However, because of the adverse publicity it received in the press I knew of it in advance, and came in by way of the swamp that runs behind the fields that were once part of the farm, and the cranberry bog that abuts them.

It was a route which I had taken before, one fateful night long, long ag—-forty-one years ago in fact.

Even in those days the house was in pretty bad shape, though it could have been saved. It could still have been saved twenty, or maybe even fifteen years ago, but in the present year, 2009, it was beyond repair, no matter what the preservations have said. The roof had caved in; the walls and floors were rotted; mold pervaded everything, including the brickwork.

No matter. It no longer exists now, which is why I have undertaken to write this account of events that took place more than four decades ago. Perhaps it will be of interest to anyone who happens to pick up this book of New England hauntings and other strange stories. My story, I trust, falls somewhere in between. Not a haunting, exactly, but certainly, at least in my estimation, strange.

It involves a crime—if crime it was—that occurred more than two centuries ago. And a theft— if theft it was—that occurred much later, as I shall relate.

"Rather stodgy, isn't he?" Lena said, looking up from the manuscript in order to give her eyes a rest. "'As I shall relate.' Must be a college professor. I assume it's a he, though I suppose it could be a she. I see it's not signed, except with the initials R. A. Looks like a man's handwriting, though." Remembering her wine, she took a few sips before returning to the manuscript:

My paternal grandfather, to whom I was very close, spent the last few remaining months of his life in a nursing home. In the course of my visits to him I became acquainted with his roommate, a man named Joseph Hickman. Mr. Hickman, though in obvious failing physical health, retained most of his mental faculties almost to the end. Eventually, as our acquaintance grew into something akin to friendship, the garrulous old man told me the story of his life.

I will not go into details, except to say that he ran away from home—the Hickman homestead—in 1904 when he was fourteen, and thereafter lived a rough life, a drifter's life of hard labor and little pay, but not without adventure, including service in the trenches in the First World War, in the course of which he was wounded. He made no contact with his family, until around the time of the Second World War, when he wrote to his sister Molly, providing her with an address at which he could receive mail.

Again I will not go into details, except to say that brother and sister carried on a correspondence, however sporadic, by mail, for nearly thirty years. In the course of this correspondence Molly, *perhaps sensing that her own end was approaching, confided in her brother the family secret, to which only she, of the six siblings, had been made privy, by her mother, shortly before the latter's death.*

It was an extraordinary secret. So extraordinary, in fact, that I scarcely lent it credence, thinking it either an unconscious fraud on the part of the sister (for whatever reason, perhaps self-delusion brought on by her years of lonely isolation in that old farmhouse) or on the part of Mr. Hickman, who by his own admission had been wounded in the First World War and had spent a life of physical hardship and wandering, and might not be (contrary to outward appearances) of sound mind.

I will not relate the story of the family secret in the indirect manner by which it was told—or rather, half whispered—to me by Mr. Hickman, piecemeal in the nursing home, over the course of weeks. It was a secret he learned entirely through means of his sister's letters to him, for after the year 1904 the two of them never talked directly to each other, either in person or by phone.

"I wish he would shit or get off the pot," Lena said, exasperated. "Such longwindedness! Even so I must say I'm intrigued."

"If you continue reading I think you'll find it worth the time spent," Cheryl remarked, amused by her friend's impatience.

"Oh, I've no doubt of that, dear. I just need an excuse to rest my eyes for a bit. And to take another sip of this excellent wine." Having taken an ample swig (more akin to a gulp than a sip), she continued her perusal:

74

The Hickman family secret was this: in 1778, during the Revolutionary War, Jabez Hickman found himself one of a mob of patriots (to put a polite label on what may be more aptly described as a rabble of opportunists) who burned and looted the stately Middleborough mansion of the prominent Tory Judge Peter Oliver.

While his fellow looters were busy carrying off furniture, carpets, and other bulky items, Jabez occupied himself by ransacking ladies' bedrooms in search of more lucrative plunder. It was a search that nearly cost him his life, in that he became trapped in the flames, but though badly burned, managed to escape only seconds after stumbling upon a secret chamber in which was concealed a small ebony casket.

Snatching the casket (which was locked) from the flames he carried it, though its contents were of considerable weight, under his arm unseen in the dark all the way to where he had tethered his horse, and rode with it home where, his wounds being attended to by his wife, he broke open the casket, which he found to be laden with jewelry and gold and silver coins.

The rest of the Hickman story grows somewhat hazy. It is after all nothing more than oral history, passed on to one family member at a time, and only one family member, down through the generations, and therefore subject to faulty memory and distortion. Furthermore, whatever level of intellect Jabez Hickman possessed (on the evidence, not high), the final two generations of his descendants were apparently lacking in both education and native intelligence (to the truth of which supposition, in the instance of my grandfather's roommate, old Joseph, I can readily attest).

Jabez, however, was shrewd enough to not only keep the secret of his find to himself, but to refrain from attempting to spend the coins or sell the jewelry, even though to a farmer on a hardscrabble New England farm it represented a vast fortune, enough to make him wealthy for life, and then some.

Unlike many of his neighbors Jabez, it seems, was no patriot; at least I can find no record of his having served in the Revolution in any capacity, Minute Man or otherwise. History tells us that only one third of the American population were in favor of breaking away from England; one third were firm loyalists, Tories like Judge Oliver; and the other third were indifferent—couldn't care less either way. Jabez, it is my belief, fell into that latter third. Rather than brand himself a traitor (should the British prevail) by making it known that he had been one of the mob who vandalized and ransacked the Oliver mansion, he kept a low profile for the remaining years of the war, waiting to see which side would emerge victorious.

By the time the British surrendered he had learned the virtue of patience. In the hard economic times that followed the war, he dipped into his treasure-trove frugally, spending one gold coin at a time, probably only a few in his entire lifetime, traveling by packet from Plymouth to Boston to do so, in order to maintain anonymity. The remainder of the coins and jewelry he kept well hidden, in a secret compartment in the kitchen, his intention being to pass the treasure on to his eldest son, so that he too could draw on it when needed, but only as much as was necessary to maintain the farm, in the hope that he in turn would do the same with his eldest son, and with the same expectation.

And this, according to the story old Joseph told me, is exactly what happened. It strains credulity, to believe that so many generations of Hickmans would show restraint, would not undertake to spend the treasure all at once, would not abandon the hard life of a New England farmer in exchange for luxury and comfort. Perhaps it was a deep-rooted Puritan ethic, or family pride in maintaining one of the oldest continuous family farms, not only in Massachusetts, but in all of New England. Or just plain superstition. Perhaps Jabez put a curse on the treasure, on any one of his descendants who would use it for any other purpose than maintaining the farm intact through good times and bad.

Or perhaps the whole story was pure fabrication, a hoax, which is what a rational person would undoubtedly believe. I, however, in my youth was not an entirely rational person. I believed the story, or half believed it, my faith in its truthfulness enough to propel me outdoors one miserable rainy night to risk life and limb—traveling through rough terrain armed only with a flashlight, to see for

*myself if the treasure was still there, if indeed it
had ever existed.*

As the narrator of a Victorian novel might say…

Here Lena could not resist breaking off reading to glance up
at her friend and quip: "The man is unquestionably an English
teacher, dear. He reminds me of you, you know, whenever you
sound professorial."

"I don't know whether to take that as a compliment or a slur,"
Cheryl, who had been quietly contemplating the fire all the while
that Lena was reading the manuscript, said, but with a smile.

"Neither, dear. I was merely stating a fact. Now let me finish
reading this, so that we can discuss it over a second glass of this
excellent Meiomi."

In preparation for the anticipated libation, she quaffed the
remaining dregs in her glass, then resumed reading the manuscript where she had left off:

*As the narrator of a Victorian novel might say,
'Reader, I found it.'*

"Ah, he found the treasure!" Lena exclaimed.

"Read on," was Cheryl's only comment.

Lena did so:

*That is to say, I found where the treasure had
been concealed. And the little of it that remained:
proof, in my mind at least, that a treasure of
immense value had once resided there. Wedged in
a crevice, so that only the most persistent probing
on my part revealed it, was a ring. A lady's ring
of inestimable beauty, of pure gold, encrusted*

with precious gems. I have not had it appraised, but considering its antiquity, and intrinsic worth, I would estimate its value at many thousands of dollars. No doubt tens of thousands.

No doubt, too, questions in the reader's mind abound, among them: What happened to the rest of the hoard, if that is it ever existed? What has become of the ring? What claim do I, a stranger to the Hickman family except for being a chance acquaintance of the last known surviving member, have to the ring?

Let me reply to these questions one by one. It is only conjecture on my part, but: what indeed happened to the rest of the hoard? It is my belief that whatever portion remained of it, a handful of coins, a few gems, or many, depending on how large the treasure had been to begin with and how closely it was hoarded by the succeeding generations of Hickmans, through various wars and depressions... it is my belief that Molly, growing old and alone in that isolated farmhouse, began to have misgivings about having disclosed, in a letter to her brother, the exact whereabouts of the treasure.

Suppose the letter fell into the wrong hands? Suppose her brother, drunkenly or inadvertently, revealed the secret to someone he trusted, or even to a total stranger? Might it not be prudent to remove the treasure to another, more secret location, a location known only to herself?

That, I believe, is what she did, unintentionally leaving behind the ring.

Did she hope that her brother would, at long last, return home? Probably. If so, she could at that time reveal to him the new hiding place. In the meantime, in a location known to no one but herself, it was safe from thieving hands.

Ah, you ask: What about your thieving hands, R. A.? What right did you have to break into the house (for that is what I did) in the first place? And having discovered the ring, what right do you have to retain possession of it, if that is what in fact you did?

My hand grows tired [the script was indeed becoming crabbed, Lena noted] *and I am running out of white space on which to write. Let others argue the ethics of the matter. The statute of limitations has run out on the "theft" of the ring, so I feel safe in revealing that I have passed it on to my eldest daughter who, I might say, knows nothing of its provenance.*

Here, abruptly, the manuscript ended.

CHAPTER XI

Lena Ponders

"So we have two mysteries now," Lena remarked. She sat at the breakfast table across from Cheryl, a steaming bowl of oat bran cereal, sans the accustomed sprinkled brown sugar, untouched before her.

Truth be told, she felt a bit crapulous this a.m. Maybe a smidgen of wine too much the evening before? She would rather die of course than admit this to Cheryl. To herself, even. But… perhaps she should abstain for a day or two? After all, she had only the one liver. Fortunately it was Cheryl who, having arisen before Lena, had spooned out Marmalade's odoriferous cat food: a task to which Lena, in her present condition, might not have been equal.

"You haven't touched your cereal," Cheryl observed.

"I'm waiting for it to cool, dear."

"You'll feel better once you've put something into your stomach," Cheryl said sympathetically.

"I feel perfectly chipper this morning," Lena insisted. To prove the fact, she consumed three spoonfuls of cereal in quick succession. And indeed felt better for it. Now, if her head would only stop aching…

"And what might one of those two mysteries be?" Cheryl inquired. "The whereabouts of your dentures? Have you misplaced them?"

Lena glared at her friend. As Cheryl well knew, she did not wear dentures. On the contrary, Lena took pride in the fact that in her mid seventies she still possessed all thirty-two—she would gladly open her mouth and allow anyone who cared to to count them (having first brushed them; she might be growing dotty in her old age but she still possessed a sense of decorum)—of her own God-given teeth.

"I'm sorry, Lena," Cheryl said with a soft laugh. "I shouldn't tease you when you're feeling under the weather." Before the older woman could protest, she added: "Seriously, what two mysteries? One I can guess: how did this Peter Gilbert come to be where he was during the nor'easter? But the second...?"

"Why, what became of the Hickman treasure?" Lena retorted, somewhat peevishly.

"Do you actually believe that story?"

"Don't you?"

"It could be R. A.'s idea of a joke. Though, to be honest, I think he really did find that ring."

"So his story rings true?" Lena asked with an air of innocence.

Cheryl made a point of groaning. "If you can pun, it at least shows that you're feeling better." She devoted a minute or two to eating her own breakfast, which consisted of a coddled egg and one slice of whole-grain toast.

"I wonder..." Lena mused.

"Wonder what?"

"If there's a connection between the two mysteries?"

"Connection? How can there be?" She shrugged. "They share no common factors. Nothing that links them, other than the fact that this Peter Gilbert and his girlfriend what's-her-name bought the old Hickman home site. We know for a fact that the house, where the treasure was allegedly hidden, was deliberately burned to the ground and the charred remains bulldozed before the land was sold."

"Even so," Lena persisted, "I don't believe in coincidences."

Cheryl, applying her napkin to her lips, repeated her shrug.

Glancing at the kitchen clock she said: "Oops. Time to go." She rose from the table. "Oh, and I won't be home for supper. I'm picking Anthony up in Onset and then we're going out for dinner. A Portuguese restaurant, I think. In New Bedford or Fall River." She gave her tummy a rueful pat. "Perhaps I should marry the man. At least if I cooked for him I could choose something light once in awhile."

"Careful, dear. If you marry him he might do all the cooking. We both know that he's an excellent cook. Especially when it comes to Cape Verdean cuisine. Lots of calories."

Cheryl dashed upstairs to her room to fetch her winter coat. As she hurried down on her way out Lena called to her from the kitchen. "What do you know of this Judge Peter Oliver, whose house Jabez Hickman helped ransack?"

Cheryl poked her head into the kitchen. "Next to nothing. Just that he was a prominent Tory and that he lived in Middleborough."

Lena was about to comment, but seeing that her friend was in a hurry merely said: "Well, drive carefully, dear. Say hello to Anthony for me tonight."

"I will," Cheryl promised. "And I'll bring leftovers home for Marmalade. Especially if we go to Antonio's. Even Anthony can't finish the gargantuan portions they serve."

Lena filled the void left by Cheryl's departure by finishing her oat bran and then pouring herself a cup of coffee. She felt better now, both her stomach and her head. She was tempted to take her coffee into the library, build a fire, and spend the morning reading.

Mentally she shook her head, rejecting the temptation. She had work to do. After cleaning up the kitchen dishes she would do a bit of laundry, then head into the center of Middleborough.

She had a date to keep. With a judge.

Lena chose a quiet corner in the reading room of the Middleborough Public Library in which to conduct her research. The reference librarian, an attractive woman in early middle age, was kind enough not only to personally select a number of books for Lena to peruse, but also to carry them to the table for her.

The books formed a formidable pile: general histories, such as *Middleborough Through the Ages* and *History of the Town of Middleboro Massachusetts* (no one, historians and town officials alike, seemed able or willing to come to a consensus concerning a standardized spelling for the name of the town), the latter in two thick volumes; and a number of more specialized books, such as *History of South Middleborough*. All proved interesting one way or another, but it was the first volume, by Thomas Weston, of the two-volume *History of the Town of Middleboro Massachusetts,* covering the period 1669-1905, which proved most useful.

Judge Peter Oliver, it turned out, had been quite a prominent figure in his day. As Chief Justice of the Massachusetts Supreme Court, he was the most powerful man, after the governor, in the Colony.

Powerful, and wealthy.

His mansion in Middleborough encompassed many acres. "Oliver Hall was built after the style of an old English mansion,"

Weston wrote, "with steep roof and deep, jutting eaves, with walls of white plaster and portico of oak, over which grew a rose not only celebrated for its beauty, but valued as a present to Madam Oliver from England. The doors and much of the inside furnishings were sent from London. The house contained the usual drawing-room of that period, the entrance-hall, the dining-room, a large and valuable library, and other apartments, with kitchen and extensive quarters for servants."

What she had read so far lent credence to R. A.'s otherwise fantastical story, Lena reflected. Such a house might well have contained hidden valuables. She read on:

"The large hall opened on the river; the lower part of the wall was wainscoted with English oak, and the upper part was decorated with rich hangings of birds and flowers." If the British had won the war, Lena chuckled to herself, it would not have been birds and flowers hanging on the wall, but instead the bodies of American patriots.

"The oaken door was polished daily by the servants until it fairly shone, and was so slippery that it is said one of the maids slipped and fell, spilling the hot tea and cream over the beautiful gown of one of the ladies and staining her white satin slipper, whereupon the enraged guest from Boston 'drew off the slipper and spanked her soundly, in high dudgeon.'"

My how times have changed, Lena thought. If that servant slipped and fell today, she would first have the 'guest from Boston' brought up on charges of assault and battery, and then sue her employer for negligence, doing all this while collecting Workers' Compensation checks. It's a good thing for the working class that the patriots won the war.

She returned her attention to the matter at hand. "The furnishings of the hall were elegant and costly; there were crownback tapestry-cushioned chairs, with a Turkish carpet on the floor."

She skipped a few passages, then continued. "The dining-room was spacious, with a large, heavy, claw-foot table of English oak in the centre, with high straight-back chairs of the same wood, the royal arms carved at the top." And on and on. I get the picture, Lena said to herself.

But what about the ransacking?

She read further until she came to the following passages: "On the breaking out of the Revolution, Judge Oliver conscientiously adhered to his sovereign, and his great wealth, his official position and influence, made him extremely obnoxious to the patriots, and in the troublesome time following the battle of Lexington ["troublesome time"—what a quaint way of describing the American Revolution! Lena thought], notwithstanding his high character and the universal respect in which he was held, he was impeached for receiving a salary from the Crown, and compelled to leave the country, with many other tories.

"After the mob had attacked the house of his brother [Andrew, who was lieutenant governor] in Boston and destroyed its contents, he rode on horseback, unattended, from Boston to Middleboro, and arrived there in the edge of the evening, travel-stained and weary. He immediately entered the Hall, where he had spent so many happy years, went to a secret drawer [ah, hidden treasure!], took out a box of valuables, cast a longing glance about, bade the faithful housekeeper good-bye, and mounting his horse, galloped out into the night."

She skimmed through the next paragraph or two. Poor Judge Peter Oliver never returned to Middleborough (for some reason, Lena preferred that variation for the spelling of the name of the town—it seemed more elegant); he sailed shortly thereafter for London, never to return to America. *Sic transit gloria mundi*, Lena reflected, unaware that decades earlier Ross Ashley (R. A.) had silently recited that same Latin sentence in reference to the passing of the Hickman dynasty.

But…if Judge Peter Oliver had removed his box of valuables from a secret drawer before fleeing Middleborough, what was it that Jabez Hickman had found? Perhaps she might find a clue elsewhere in the book.

She flipped a few pages until she came to the following: "Mrs. Mary Norcutt, when a young woman, was the housekeeper at Oliver Hall, and lived in the family of Judge Weston [ancestor of Thomas Weston, the author of the very book she was holding in her hands]. She was very fond of giving a description of the place, the parties, incidents and prominent men who were accustomed to visit there. These incidents were often told to the father of the writer, and an account of the burning of the hall as she used to relate it was written by the late Granville T. Sproat:

"We had long expected that the Hall would be burned—the people were so enraged; especially after we heard how they had sacked Governor Hutchinson's house in Boston, and had brought out and burned all his fine library of books in the street. We never went to bed at night without thinking that we should be aroused before morning by the Hall being on fire.

"And it was so. One night, a little past midnight, we were awakened by a loud knocking at the door, and a cry, 'Get up! get up! the Hall is on fire!' We sprang up; we could see the Hall from our windows; the main building was not then on fire; it was the library which was connected with the Hall by a latticed gallery, that was all in a blaze. We ran out to the Hall; a good many people had got there; they had broken in the doors and were running through the building with the hopes of finding something to lay their hands on."

Lena skipped a few more passages until: "I then ran into the great parlor, to the money closet. It stood open. I put my hand in one corner of a shelf; there was a piece of money about the size of a dollar. I took it home with me and kept it for years afterwards...The Hall was a long time burning. It was covered with plaster of some kind on the outside, and did not burn very fast. The roof kept falling in, one part after another. It was a long time before the guest parlor was burnt out."

Lena set the book aside. She had read all the pertinent passages.

It was time now to weigh the evidence.

Was R. A.'s story, scribbled in longhand on the flyleaves of a book, a true account, or a hoax?

There was no way of knowing for sure. He—the author was a he, she felt certain—might have been having his little joke at the expense of gullible readers of books of New England hauntings. But would anyone go to all that trouble, to make the whole thing up, in the off chance that whoever purchased the book, from whatever second-hand source, would read it and be duped?

She didn't think so. Despite the pun, the story did have the ring of truth. It could have happened the way R. A. heard it from old Joe Hickman. History was on the side of probability. It was an historical fact that Judge Oliver's house had been ransacked and burned. In her memoir, the housekeeper mentioned that it had burned slowly—allowing time for Jabez Hickman to seek out secreted valuables, though in the event he had been badly burned.

But—if the whole thing was a hoax, had R. A. conceived the idea for it after reading the housekeeper's memoir? "I put my hand in one corner of a shelf; there was a piece of money about the size of a dollar," she had written. R. A.—or so he claimed— had put his hand into a secret cupboard of the Hickman farmhouse. And pulled out a gold ring.

Too close a similarity?

Lena sighed. There was no way of telling.

And yet, having weighed the evidence, her intuition told her that the story of the Hickman secret, however improbable, was real.

All that remained now was to find a link between the lost treasure of the Hickmans, and the unexplained death of the landscaper Peter Gilbert.

CHAPTER XII

Artisans of Death

Though the parking lot at the funeral home appeared to be full (a repletion aided and abetted by mounds of snow heaped up after the last storm), several cars were leaving as Frank arrived; he quickly found a space for his pickup, even as a half dozen vehicles pulled into the lot behind him. More than one wake was being held, it seemed. Even so, he guessed that the lion's share of the visitors were for Peter Gilbert's.

Peter had been in the landscaping business for a number of years, since before Frank first met him. Because of his affability, his open nature, his generosity and physical courage (which Frank had witnessed, indeed been beneficiary of), as well as his professional integrity, he had made a lot of friends in his lifetime.

And then there was the mystery surrounding Peter's death, along with the widespread publicity it had received. Not a few of the so-called mourners might be little more than bored thrill seekers, attracted by morbid curiosity, acquaintances or even strangers who might not otherwise have bothered to come.

Speaking of which—wasn't that Lena Lombardi's black sedan, there a couple of spaces over? He recognized it because of the dented front left fender, a dent which Lena claimed had been caused by a lamp post coming in contact with the automobile in the parking lot of the Silver City Galleria. She would have the dent removed in the spring, she had told him, when parking lots were no longer slick with ice, a condition which made parking next to lamp posts not only difficult, but hazardous as well.

The funeral home parking lot, scraped down to the bare pavement and liberally coated with coarse sand, posed no such hazard; the owners probably figured, with no shortage of corpses likely to occur in the predictable future, they had no need to create cadavers on the way in.

Frank entered through the main door (better that, than the delivery door in the rear) where he was greeted by an obsequious young man impeccably dressed in a somber gray suit, who when Frank mouthed the word "Gilbert" directed him to the parlor on the left.

Frank's surmise proved correct. The bulk of the cars in the lot outside could be accounted for by the occupants of this one parlor. Before crossing the threshold he took a moment to survey the room. Only a handful of the seats in the dozen or more rows facing the bier on which the coffin reposed were empty, though most mourners (or in at least one notable instance, *spectators*), having already offered their condolences at the reception line, remained seated only a short while, just long enough to show respect.

Lena occupied a seat in a row well to the rear. When Frank attempted to make eye contact she glanced away, taking a sudden interest in a potted plant in a far corner of the room. What cat-and-mouse game was she up to this time? he wondered. Why not go whole hog and come disguised? Nothing so crass as a Groucho Marx mustache with horn-rimmed glasses and bulbous nose, perhaps. But a wig of flaming red hair, lipstick of a similarly garish shade, inch-thick eyeshadow, and stiletto heels for added measure, might have done the trick.

Oh well. His friend was incorrigible. He would play the game her way, pretend not to know her. They could compare notes afterwards. While sharing, of course, the inevitable bottle of wine.

His eyes next fell on a figure in a row mid center: that of Detective Benjamin Andrade of the Rochester Police Department. The lanky detective appeared lost in thought, contemplating, perhaps, the vicissitudes of human existence, or, given the occasion, pondering the likelihood, its pros and cons, of a continuation of that existence after death.

Either he did not notice Frank's entrance, or he pretended not to.

Detective Andrade too, it seemed, was playing at cat-and-mouse, scoping out the wake's attendees: a tried and true ploy of the constabulary, attending the murdered victim's obsequies in hopes that the killer would show up and in some way, however insignificant, betray him- or herself.

So—Andrade was not satisfied with the assumption that Peter Gilbert's death had been accidental. What would the detective make of Frank's presence at the wake?

Frank got in line. There were five or six mourners in front of him, kneeling before the coffin or offering words of comfort to the bereaved. These latter stood in two distinct groupings, somewhat apart from one another. The first group consisted of two men and two women: as Frank in due course discovered, Peter's brother and sister and their respective spouses. He exchanged a few appropriate words with them and moved on to the second group.

Even though nearly two decades had elapsed since he last laid eyes on her—two decades that had not treated her kindly—Frank had no difficulty recognizing Beatrice Souza. He recalled describing her to Lena. What were the words he had chosen? *Pretty in a chunky sort of way.*

For a woman in her mid to late forties she was still attractive, he supposed, though she could not hold a candle to his wife, Laura, who after bearing two children still retained her figure. Not so Beatrice—who, to his knowledge, was childless. She was not obese, exactly, not by today's standards. But chunkiness had deliquesced to flab, and her once pretty features had somehow coarsened. He couldn't quite put his finger on it. Her complexion? That might be part of it. The rich olive had dulled, to take on a jaundiced tone. She dyed her hair, that was obvious. She used too much makeup. Her chin was beginning to sag...

Why, Frank reproached himself, was he judging the poor woman so harshly? As he moved closer to Beatrice he took note of her demeanor, her posture, the expression in her eyes—and understood the reason why she evoked his censure.

She was not in mourning.

Peter Gilbert's siblings exhibited true grief; despite an outward composure there was sadness in their eyes. Beatrice, on the other hand, although she made a show of dabbing her eyes with a moist handkerchief, and spoke in low, mournful tones, rather than being distressed, seemed almost—this was just a gut feeling, but as a former law enforcement officer he had learned to trust his gut—lighthearted, buoyant, as if the loss of her lover was nothing more than the welcome closing of one chapter and the opening of another.

Or was Frank being too harsh on the woman? He was, after all, biased. He had never cared for Beatrice Souza. From the very outset of his fraud investigation twenty years ago he had pegged her as self-centered, dishonest, no fit companion for a decent fellow like Peter Gilbert.

And yet she must possess some good qualities; the poor man had been besotted with her. Let him who is without sin cast the first stone...

Abruptly, it seemed to Frank, all eyes were upon him.

Nonsense. How many here, in this room (other than Detective Andrade, Lena Lombardi, and Beatrice Souza), recognized him as the man upon whose property Peter Gilbert's body had been mysteriously found? Found by him. Frank Gallerani. The man upon whose property Peter Gilbert's body had been mysteriously found.

The phrase kept repeating itself. The man upon whose property…Why in hell's blazes am I attending this wake? he asked himself.

To pay his condolences to the deceased's girlfriend, of course. To show respect for the man who had saved his life that fateful day on the waterfront, when Frank was about to receive—compliments of Jack "The Rat" Bartlett and his two lumper cronies—unwanted alterations to his anatomy by means of an ice pick. A complete makeover.

He was here for another reason, too: to come to grips with the fact that he remained, in the eyes of the police and of others, under a cloud—a cloud that would not lift until the presence of Peter Gilbert's body lying half frozen on the lonely road that led to Frank's house could be satisfactory explained.

Beatrice was not alone. Next to her stood a much older woman whose grief seemed genuine; her eyes were red from weeping. She was dressed entirely in black, from the top of her head to the tip of her toes: widow's weeds, of a style still fashionable in certain regions of southern Europe. Whiskers sprouted between the wrinkles of her chin—Marmalade would have been envious; and above her lips the outlines of a mustache were clearly visible.

The woman was obviously Portuguese, born and bred there, widowed there too, mayhap. A recent immigrant to America.

A relative of Beatrice?

Before he had a chance to speak Beatrice beat him to the punch: "Mr. Gallerani. I didn't expect *you* here. Although," she added quickly, "it's kind of you to come. Pete always thought highly of you."

"And I of him," Frank said. "I'm truly sorry about…what happened to him."

She looked him square in the eye. "Detective Andrade says you have no idea why Pete should have been walking down the road to your house during that northeaster. Is that true?"

He nodded. "I'm afraid so. No idea whatsoever."

"It'll forever remain a mystery, I suppose," Beatrice said, lowering her eyes in what Frank assumed was an attempt to appear demure. "Oh, let me introduce you to my aunt Inês Gonsalves."

She spoke a few words in Portuguese to her aunt: an explanation, Frank guessed, of who he was.

"How do you do, Senhora?" Frank said politely. "I'm sorry we have to meet under such sad circumstance."

Senhora Gonsalves nodded. "He was a good man," she said, in heavily accented English. "A good man." She directed her eyes at her niece. "You will miss him, Beatrice." She said it almost as an accusation, as if to imply—or was Frank again imagining things?—that her niece had not appreciated the great good fortune she had when her man was alive.

There followed an awkward silence. Frank, who could think of nothing appropriate to say, was rescued by the knot of mourners behind him and the necessity to move on.

He paused before the open casket. The morticians had done an admirable job of making the corpse appear natural, as if Peter Gilbert had suffered no more than a minor bruise to the head. Frank bowed his own in silent prayer. He did not direct his words to a god in whose existence he did not believe, but rather to Peter

Gilbert, words of thanks for the man who had, many years ago, saved him from a nasty situation.

As for nasty situations…he could sense Detective Andrade's gaze boring like a gimlet into his back.

He stood with bowed head for several minutes before moving beyond the coffin. He took his time, so as to admire the abundance of flower arrangements sent by friends and acquaintances of the deceased, artfully placed around the coffin so that it seemed to float on a sea of bloom.

He had to credit the morticians: they were true artisans of death.

Turning at last, Frank directed his own gaze—ignoring that of the detective—up and down the rows of seats, as if seeking a convenient place in which to sit. Lena chose that moment to once again take an inordinate interest in the potted plant at the far end of the room. Are you considering acquiring a similar plant for a favored spot in your living room? he would ask her, at the first opportunity. Much as he liked Lena, he did enjoy roughing up her feathers once in a while.

The first row of seats, he noticed, was almost entirely taken up by men, and a few women, who, judging by their callused hands and sun-darkened complexions, spent much of their time outdoors doing manual labor. Men and women employed by Peter in his landscaping business, or by Beatrice at the nursery, he assumed.

One of them in fact looked familiar.

A short man—scarcely five feet two, his complexion dark by nature as well as by the ministrations of the sun. Central American, of mostly Indian ancestry, Frank guessed. Or was it memory that prompted him? That was it. The man had worked for Peter Gilbert, had in fact been Peter's helper on the job he did for Frank, the landscaping Laura had insisted on when they moved in to the antique house by the cranberry bog, and the repairs to the old stone wall.

Pedro? No, not Pedro. Pablo. That was it. The man's name was Pablo. Guatemalan, if memory served. Peter had spoken highly of him, as a hard and loyal worker. He had also hinted that Pablo was here in the States illegally. Peter though basically honest had not, at least in this one instance, balked at hiring illegals.

Some of Beatrice's venality had apparently rubbed off, after all.

Although…there was an alternative, an exculpatory explanation. Maybe Peter had simply felt sorry for Pablo. Maybe he had not wanted to see a decent, hardworking man, a refugee from poverty or oppression, deported, and had helped keep him safe by employing him these many years.

Pablo must have felt Frank's gaze upon him, for he glanced his way. Their eyes met. Pablo recognized him, of that Frank was certain. He let his eyes linger upon Frank a moment or two before finally averting his gaze elsewhere.

Frank caught two mourners in the front row staring at him. A man and a woman, they stood out from their fellows because of their close resemblance to one another, and their dissimilarity from the others—brother and sister surely, if not actual twins (he guessed their age at somewhere around forty)—their blond hair bleached almost white by the sun, their naturally fair skin bronzed a deep auburn by exposure to sun, wind and rain.

He felt a degree of hostility in their stare. Did they recognize him, hold him somehow responsible for their boss's death? After a moment or two they abruptly left off staring, as if by telepathic accord.

Only then did Frank direct his eyes toward where Andrade was sitting. This time the detective not only met his gaze but held it, and nodded. Was the nod meant merely to acknowledge

Frank's presence? Or was it intended to convey something more sinister? Something to the effect that, *Yes, Mr. Gallerani, you have not disappointed. I was after all expecting you.*

Frank changed his mind about remaining a while longer; he decided to leave immediately. He crossed the room to the doorway. Just inside it the unctuous young man had taken up position beside a mahogany table. As Frank approached the young man made a gesture toward the table, on which was displayed a large guest register, bound in leather, similar to the type once commonly found in hotels, in the days before computers. It was open, split down the middle like a gutted fish.

"Have you signed the register, sir?"

Frank shook his head. "I hadn't planned on checking in," he was tempted to say, but refrained. Under the circumstances the joke was in poor taste; besides, the young man would not understand the allusion anyhow.

He took up the pen and signed his name, in large bold letters, then took the opportunity to scan the names preceding his. Had Lena used a pseudonym, a *nom de guerre?* he wondered.

No, there it was, on the preceding page: *Lena Lombardi,* in neat, ornate cursive, a reflection of the days when the art of fine penmanship was regularly taught in schools. Just above Lena's signature was that of Benjamin Andrade. In contrast to Lena's, "Ben's" signature was a hasty scrawl, barely legible. There were dozens of names in the register, demonstrating once again the high esteem in which Peter Gilbert had been held.

Frank sought out one additional entry, and found it, on the first page: *Pablo Morales.* That, he assumed, was a made-up name—if the man was in fact an illegal alien. The other names in the register meant nothing to him.

He exited the building into the parking lot. The sun's rays, though slanting, had warmed the air and melted some of the snow. As he crossed the lot to his car he heard the sound of approaching footsteps behind him.

"Señor Gallerani!"

The man he knew as Pablo Morales hurried toward him. "You are Señor Gallerani, no?"

Frank nodded. "Your name is Pablo, I believe. You worked for Mr. Gilbert."

"Si, señor. For many years."

"You were his helper when he did a job on my property, a number of years ago."

"Si. That is how I know your name. When I see it in the newspaper, how you find Mr. Gilbert in the snow, I remember. Mr. Gilbert, he liked you."

"I liked him too, Pablo."

Pablo grasped the sleeve of Frank's woolen coat and tugged at it. "Mr. Gallerani, I must talk to you."

Taken aback by Pablo's sudden gesture, Frank hesitated, then said: "Certainly. What is it you want to say?"

Pablo held on tight to the loose folds of Frank's sleeve, as if needing its support to keep his balance. For a moment he said nothing, just stared at Frank, as if at a loss for words—appalled at his own temerity.

"What is it?" Frank asked, with the patience he had learned in his years as a special investigator.

Pablo maintained his hold on Frank's sleeve but said nothing.

We must present quite a tableau to any passersby, Frank thought, standing here like mute statues in the middle of the funeral home parking lot.

When finally Pablo spoke it was in a near whisper. "You were once a policeman, is that not so?"

"A type of policeman, yes," Frank said. "That's how I met Peter—Mr. Gilbert. He did me a great favor once."

"You are no longer a policeman?"

"No."

Pablo breathed a sigh of relief, and let go of Frank's sleeve. "I did not think so. But I had be sure."

"I think I understand," Frank said. If Pablo was an illegal he would naturally not want to become involved with the police. "So what is it you want to tell me, Pablo?"

"You must tell no one that it is I who tell you this," Pablo insisted.

"You haven't told me anything yet," Frank pointed out. "But don't worry. I know how to keep a secret."

Pablo nodded. "I trust you." He spoke softly, as if even though the parking lot was deserted except for the two of them he was fearful of being overheard. He leaned closer to Frank. "Mr. Gilbert—his death was not an accident."

"Not an accident? How can that be?" Frank asked.

Out of the corner of his eye he saw someone emerge from the funeral parlor: Lena Lombardi. And close behind her, Detective Andrade. Pablo spied the two at about the same time. Whatever it was he had been about to reveal to Frank remained unspoken.

"I speak to you later," he murmured.

"Wait. It's only…"

Before Frank could complete the sentence Pablo broke away. Like a cartoon character pursued by villains he wove a frantic path between the parked vehicles to a beat-up Toyota Corolla at the far end of the lot. Frank watched as he hastily scrambled into the front passenger side. There he remained huddled, with his head down, like a small child hiding from a bully.

Old habits die hard. For no particular reason Frank made a mental note of the license plate number.

Then, rather than stand there with his mouth agape, he headed toward his own vehicle. As he climbed into the cab he glanced behind him. Lena, the picture of innocence and unconcern, strolled serenely toward her sedan. Andrade, on the other hand, stood gazing in his direction with a bemused expression on his face, like someone examining the pieces of a jigsaw puzzle, hoping to find the missing piece that would make sense of the whole.

CHAPTER XIII
Grave Discussion

Frank drove home.

As he passed the spot where he'd found Peter Gilbert's lifeless body lying in the snow he felt a sudden compulsion to hit the gas pedal and speed on by. Instead he slammed on the brakes and got out of the pickup. Head bowed, he stood in the shadows by the side of the dirt track, feeling the cold, listening to the wind moan through the branches of the bare trees.

When would Peter's ghost cease to haunt the site?

It was a rhetorical question. Frank knew all too well the answer: when the mystery of his death was solved.

"How did it go?" Laura asked, as Frank slid out of his winter coat and accepted the steaming cup of coffee she had poured for him even before he entered the house.

He told her: about Beatrice, about Lena, about Andrade, about Pablo Morales.

"I can tell you're worried," she said, though there was no undue concern in her voice. They were seated at the kitchen table. The living room, with its Franklin stove, would have been cozier, but Frank had plunked himself down at the kitchen table and there they remained. The coffee pot, at least, was readily at hand.

"Not so much worried as…I don't know. Disturbed, I guess."

"Let's go over what you've told me," Laura suggested, "then see whether there's any reason why you should be…worried, or disturbed, or whatever."

Today was one of her rare free days. She often worked nights; on such occasions she slept as best she could by day, but this twenty-four-hour cycle was her own, to do as she pleased. She was dressed comfortably, in slacks, a blouse, and a sweater her cousin Kate had knitted her as a Christmas present a few years back.

"Let's consider the principle players in this one-act play. I hope you'll pardon the analogy, but that's what it sounded like, Frank."

He smiled. "I suppose the whole thing does come across as melodramatic."

"A little. Anyhow, let's begin with Beatrice Souza."

She got up from her chair, went over to a cupboard, and took down a bottle of Johnny Walker Red. "This calls for something a little stronger than mere coffee." She poured them each a dollop. "Hmm. Scotch and coffee. Not a bad combination. It's a good thing the girls are doing a sleep-over tonight. I wouldn't want them here to see their parents soused."

Frank grunted, in his present mood the closest he could get to a chuckle.

"Your gut feeling is that Beatrice wasn't overly upset by the loss of her—what should we call him?—her lover, her partner. Well, that's not a crime."

"Not in itself, no," Frank agreed.

"As for Lena Lombardi being there, we both know that… well, let's face it, she's a…how can I describe her?…a busybody. She's bored, and thinks she's the twenty-first century's answer to

Sherlock Holmes."

"True. But I trust her instincts. She's a shrewd woman. If she smells a rat, then there's at least a rodent present, even if it's just a mouse. I find it hard to believe that it was mere curiosity that brought her to the funeral home today, or that caused her to act as if she and I are total strangers."

"She's been watching too many old black-and-white movies," Laura said. "Film noir and cloak-and-dagger stuff. Or she read too many Nancy Drew mysteries as a child." She shrugged. "I think we can dismiss Lena for now. Let's move on to the next person on your list: Detective Andrade. He's got you paranoid. Sure, he's suspicious. But of what? Why Peter Gilbert's dead body should have shown up on our road hasn't been satisfactorily explained. That still doesn't make his death anything but accidental. What are you so…disturbed…about?"

"Mainly, Pablo Morales," Frank said.

He drained his cup and held it out for a refill. Laura obliged, by filling their cups part way with the remainder of the coffee, then topping them off with a liberal application of scotch.

"Peter Gilbert's death was not an accident. That's what he claims?"

Frank nodded.

"But Frank, that doesn't mean anything. The man's upset at the death of his employer." She sipped her fortified coffee. "He has reason to be upset, if he truly is in this country illegally. True, he can always get another job. On the bogs, if nowhere else. But the work will be a lot harder and the pay not very good. He may be sending money home to support family members in, what is it, Venezuela?"

"Guatemala."

"In any case, he'll no longer have Peter to shield him from possible deportation. So, sure he's upset, and that's made him suspicious, paranoid even."

Frank shook his head. "Everything you say is true, but it doesn't account for the way he behaved. Pablo Morales is scared, and not just of possible deportation. He knows something, I'm sure of it."

Laura took a deep sigh. "If you think that's the case, Frank, then I admit you're probably right." She got up from her chair, went over to his, and planted a kiss on his cheek. "You were a topnotch investigator; I shouldn't question your judgment." She returned to her chair and sipped at her drink.

"But you don't want me to get involved, and I don't blame you," Frank said, after taking a series of liberal sips from his. "The reason we bought this place was to get away from all that. We both agree we have the girls to think about. Who was it who said, When you have children, you have given hostages to fate?"

"Someone wise," Laura said.

"So I won't get involved," Frank said. "Not directly. Except for one thing."

"Pablo Morales. You'll question him."

"Yes. I've jotted down the license plate number of the vehicle he got into. I still have friends in the Bureau who owe me favors. If Pablo doesn't contact me in a day or two, I'll find out from them where he lives and pay him a visit. I owe that much to Peter."

"And that's it?"

He nodded. "That's it. I promise. With the possible exception, of course," he added with a sly grin that would put the Cheshire cat to shame, "of enlisting the aid of my good friend, Lena Lombardi."

CHAPTER XIV
By the Lake

The tan Toyota Corolla in which the skittish Pablo Morales had cowered at the funeral home parking lot was registered to Carlos Juan Hernandez. Mr. Hernandez's address was in Freetown, in a secluded area of modest cottages clustered on the shores of a wooded lake near the Rochester line.

When, three days after the wake, Pablo had still not contacted him, Frank made a phone call to a former colleague who was more than happy to bend the law and provide Frank with the information he needed.

"Just give me a day or two, Frank ol' buddy. I have to go in through the back door on this one, so to speak."

Two days later the phone rang and Frank was in possession of a name and address.

The owner of the Toyota, Carlos Juan Hernandez, was not connected to a land line. That suited Frank just fine; he preferred to drop in unannounced anyhow.

A towering white pine that in colonial times would have been notched with the King's Broad Arrow (thus reserving it for exclusive use by the British Navy), damaged by the fierce winds and heavy snows of the recent nor'easter, chose the day on which Frank was preparing to set out, to give up the ghost and topple onto a section of road that led through the swamp. It took Frank five hours with chain saw and front-end loader to make the road passable again.

Task completed, he tramped into the house, took a hot shower, and revisited the bottle of Johnny Walker Red that he and Laura had tapped into earlier in the week. Drink in hand, he dozed off in front of the Franklin stove.

Thus, not until some eight days had passed since the incident in the funeral home parking lot did Frank finally set out on his mission to question Pablo Morales. In the interim the weather had moderated. Though it was not yet spring, everywhere there were signs of its approach: warm temperatures, melting snow, cavity-nesting birds—woodpeckers, titmice, chickadees, white-breasted nuthatches—seeking out suitable sites in dead trees, and in the nesting boxes Frank had erected here and there, within view of the house.

The street on which the exotic bird Carlos Juan Hernandez had established his nesting box was one of a handful of graveled tracks off of which, shortly after World War II, blue collar workers had erected for themselves summer cottages (some scarcely more than shacks) fronting a diminutive lake that was just big enough to accommodate a rickety wooden pier for the launching of boats and a pebble beach for the kids. Since then the area had been gentrified: the cottages spruced up, several winterized, the shacks enlarged or torn down.

Frank located chez Hernandez without difficulty. It was one of the few dwellings inhabited year round.

Hernandez's tan Toyota Corolla took up a third of the length of the driveway leading to a nonexistent garage next to the house. In lieu of the garage there was a fenced-in victory garden. Behind the sturdy white pickets desiccated stalks and decayed leaves of corn, cabbages, squash, cucumbers, tomatoes nosed through the half-melted snow, mute testimony to the industry of the house's occupants. In the midst of all this, stark against the blue winter sky, stood a row of naked bean poles, like the petrified legs of prehistoric shorebirds, as if this fragile lake had once been an inland sea.

Though modest, the property was professionally landscaped, by far the best groomed in the neighborhood; Carlos had put his landscaping skills to good use. Frank parked his pickup behind the Toyota and followed a neatly paved walkway to the front steps. He knocked on the door. As he stood there waiting a chill wind gusted off the lake, belying the promise of spring.

A young teenage girl opened the door. Petite, pretty, her dark hair neatly trimmed (no visible tattoos or body-piercings), she reminded Frank of his own daughters. She stood in the doorway, neither hostile nor smiling, but with an inquiring look.

"Is Mr. Hernandez in?"

The girl nodded, and turning toward the interior of the house shouted, "Dad!" Then, remembering her manners, or perhaps merely desiring to close the door to conserve heat, she invited Frank to step inside.

There was a brief delay while Hernandez finished whatever he had been doing, during which his daughter offered Frank a seat on the sofa, then left. The living room was small, proportionate to the house, clean, without clutter, the furnishing not new, but well preserved. The prints on the wall were of nature scenes.

When Hernandez emerged from the kitchen Frank recognized him as one of the men he'd seen seated up front in the funeral home parlor.

Frank stood and introduced himself. "I was a friend of Peter Gilbert's," he added, to explain the reason for his visit.

Hernandez nodded. "I saw you at the wake."

"Did Pablo Morales by any chance mention to you that he had spoken to me?"

"As a matter of fact he did. Look, why don't you sit down and I'll have Susan, my daughter, fix us some coffee. My wife, Esmeralda, is at work," he added.

"I don't want to put you to any trouble …"

"No trouble, Mr. Gallerani. I usually have coffee at this hour anyhow. Susan!"

"I've already got it going, Dad," Susan shouted from the kitchen.

Hernandez beamed. "A good girl, my Susan. Takes after her mother. And, I think, a little after me."

"She reminds me of my own girls," Frank said. "Although I can't say that Maria and Linda are as cheerful as your daughter seems to be about helping out around the house."

Susan entered carrying a tray with a pot of coffee, cups, spoons, napkins, cream and sugar. Only when his guest was served and he himself had a cup in hand did Hernandez return to the purpose of Frank's visit.

"Pablo did mention your name, Mr. Gallerani. He doesn't own a car, or have a license. He asked if I would give him a ride to your house, and I said of course." He shrugged. "We're both out of a job now, with Mr. Gilbert gone. I have plenty of time on my hands."

"I'm sure with your obvious skills—I was admiring the grounds before I came in—you won't have trouble finding work."

"Me, no. As for Palblo…" He made a gesture, equivalent to the Spanish expression, *Quien sabe?*

"I think I understand," Frank said. "With him it might be more difficult. But, what about the nursery and greenhouses? Won't Miss Souza have work for him to do?"

Hernandez studied the cup in his hand, then took a quick swallow. He set the cup down carefully on the low table in front of them. Only then did he look Frank in the eyes.

"Pablo has this thing…he doesn't like 'la Señorita Souza,' as he calls her. Mr. Gallerani, Pablo has not told me why he wanted to see you. But from the hints he dropped—he is not a subtle man—I think he believes that Miss Souza is somehow responsible for Mr. Gilbert's death."

"But how can that be?" Frank asked. "The police found no evidence of foul play."

Again Hernandez shrugged. "I can only repeat what Pablo…" He paused, then laughed. "I can only repeat what Pablo did *not* say to me. But I think I could read his mind."

"Do you think she had anything to do with Mr. Gilbert's death?" Frank asked.

"What I think doesn't matter, Mr. Gallerani. I'm just a simple working man, with a wife and two children to support. My son, Peter—I named him after Mr. Gilbert—you have not met. He is a senior in high school. On weekends he works at Market Basket."

Having deftly changed the subject, he poured Frank another cup of coffee.

"I had expected Pablo to contact me before now," Frank said. "I got the impression that what he had to say to me was urgent."

"I expected to hear from him, too," Hernandez said. "We keep in touch by cell phone. I've called him two or three times, but no answer. Maybe he's had second thoughts about talking to you."

"Maybe, " Frank agreed, but added: "Can you give me his phone number and address?"

CHAPTER XV
Déjà Vu

"It's a big house. Pretentious. A…what's the expression? a McMansion, set back maybe two hundred feet. Easy to find. This time of year you can see it from the road," Hernandez informed him.

Ten minutes after leaving Freetown Frank swung onto Snipatuit Road in Rochester.

Hernandez was right: a big house, easy to find. Long before he reached the drive Frank spotted the number, painted in white numerals on a black mailbox attached to a granite post by the side of the road.

"The owners don't live there in the winter," Hernandez informed him. "They're rich people. They own a house in Florida. Pablo, he lives in the garage. You know, an apartment on top. He looks after the place." Hernandez thought a moment before adding, "You know, I don't think that apartment is legal. That's why they let Pablo live there cheap. That's just my opinion."

Once he'd seen the apartment that became Frank's opinion, too.

The asphalt drive that cut from Snipatuit Road through a thin grove of deciduous trees had been plowed since the last storm. That made sense—the owners would contract with someone to clear it after each snowfall, not just for Pablo's sake, but also for less altruistic purposes: to deceive would-be burglars into believing that the house was occupied, and to provide access to emergency vehicles, such as fire trucks.

Frank followed the drive to the end. With a cursory glance at the house—an oversized box devoid of anything approaching architectural appeal—he pulled up in front of the three-car garage, turned, and aimed his pickup at the distant road. When he climbed out of the cab and glanced upwards it was not readily apparent that the garage had an apartment on top; the upper portion looked like nothing more than storage space. Someone, Pablo presumably, had shoveled a path through the snow, now mostly melted, around the side to the rear, where Frank found a set of stairs leading up.

He doubted whether the steep, narrow stairway would meet code. Maybe that's how the owners had become wealthy, by cutting corners, ignoring inconvenient laws and regulations.

He mounted the stairs to the landing and knocked on the door.

No answer.

He called out Pablo's name, and knocked again.

Again, silence.

Pablo could be out. He probably had friends other than Hernandez who would gladly give him a ride, take him grocery shopping or to the dentist. Or maybe he had a girlfriend and was out somewhere with her. Or maybe he had simply gone for a stroll.

Frank turned his back to the door, undecided.

From the landing he had an unobstructed view of Snipatuit Pond. The surface of the pond was mottled. In places it shone sparkling blue; in others it was marred by gray, uneven sheets of rotting ice. An ice-fisherman's crude hut, abandoned for the season, and now partially sunk, rested precariously on the shallow bottom a few feet from shore. He knocked on the door again.

Still no answer. He took out his cell phone and punched in Pablo's number, which he'd obtained from Hernandez. "Pablo doesn't answer my calls; maybe he'll answer yours," the latter had said, without conviction.

From inside the apartment there issued the sound of musical notes.

Pablo's phone, ringing.

Frank tried the door. It was unlocked. He let himself in.

He found himself in the kitchen. Pablo was a neat housekeeper. He kept the place tidy. No clutter, no dirty dishes in the sink. Just an overpowering—all too familiar—stench.

It was a small apartment: kitchen, sitting room, bedroom, bath. The fire marshall would not be happy with the layout; there was only the one entry, no alternative exit. Definitely not up to code.

Frank found the phone lying by itself on the kitchen table.

He found Pablo, also lying by himself, on the sitting room floor. Frank had been wrong; there was an alternative exit, after all: Death.

Judging from the stench, Pablo had made his exit from this world several days ago. Frank did not have to examine the body to ascertain the cause of death. Pablo's head had been bashed in. There was a pool of blood, dried to the consistency of glue, on the bare floor, splotches on the walls and ceiling.

Blood splatter. It told its own story. Frank had taken a course in it while employed by the BSI. He recognized the stains on the ceiling as droplets from the violent upswing of whatever object had repeatedly smashed Pablo's skull. He could tell by the pattern on the walls that there had been no struggle. Pablo had been struck, unawares, from behind.

"Shit."

Frank felt bad for what had happened to Pablo. But he also

felt bad for what was happening to himself. For the second time in two weeks he would have to report finding a body. How friendly would his pal "Ben" be after this?

Frank could of course just leave, drive away, pretend he'd never been here.

Under no circumstances, however, would he think of doing such a thing; he was a man of integrity (although some might call him a fool). But other than causing him to lose his self respect, failing to report the body could land him in real trouble. In the first place, someone might have seen him, or his pickup, on the property. The house was not so secluded that it didn't have neighbors. In the second, Hernandez, who as a friend and co-worker of the murdered man would be questioned, would be bound to mention Frank's visit to Freetown, and his stated intention to call on Pablo Morales. Then there was the little matter of fingerprints. Frank's would be found on the door knob, on whatever else he might have touched. And footprints in the mud.

And DNA and fibers and other telltale traces everywhere.

He took out his cell phone again. This time he had no doubt that the ring would be promptly answered.

PART TWO

These Magic Moments

CHAPTER XVI

Old Vine Zinfandel

Lena Lombardi sat at her kitchen table, a cup of black coffee—reduced now to just the dregs—at her elbow, a copy of the 20th anniversary issue of the literary journal *The Aurorean* splayed open before her. Cheryl subscribed to the journal; Lena liked to dip into it occasionally, especially when she felt a bit out of sorts: down in the dumps, as she expressed it to Cheryl. As a rule poetry—in particular nature poetry—had the power to lift her up. She wasn't too sure, though, about the poem she had just read, titled "March, Pentimento."

She read it again.

> Yesterday the pond's shell,
> paper thin, dissolved;
> now its water wrinkles.
>
> Flakes of song
> flit from trees'
> bare branches.
>
> A Mourning Cloak,
> winter's withered leaf,
> floats by.

High up, winds
scour the sky,
drive drab from blue.

The sun's sharp.
Winter erased?
Not quite.

A smudge of gray,
a smear of cloud,
remains.

All in all, a poem of transition, she decided. Winter into spring. *Pentimento*, she now knew, having looked the word up in one of the many reference books with which her library was well stocked, was a term used by painters, "the sign of a change of mind or concealed mistake by the artist in executing a picture." The artist would paint over the mistake, "but as in the course of years the covering pigment may become transparent the lower layer begins to show through," revealing the mistake, or original intention, that lay beneath.

She liked the image of the ice as the pond's shell; and the Mourning Cloak—despite its somber name, a beautiful butterfly, really: a rich brownish-maroon, with an inner border along the wings of bright blue spots, and an outer border of creamy yellow—as "winter's withered leaf." It was a favorite butterfly of hers; it might appear anytime during the year, sometimes on warm days even in the dead of winter. She had spotted them, flitting by, in past Februarys, and been cheered.

Lena read the poem once again: just that little smudge, that smear of gray cloud in an otherwise blue sky. It was, all in all, an apt description of the day, the time of year.

She set the journal aside and rose from the table to stand at the back door of her modern Greek Revival house. From there she gazed longingly toward the gazebo, at the clusters of snow-drops that had begun to bloom along the walkway even before the snow had melted, and at the myriads of crocuses that, just now daring to unfold their blossoms, would soon carpet the lawn with their bright, festive colors.

If the deer didn't eat them first.

Deer, Lena reflected, are fond of crocuses.

Thankfully, coyotes are fond of deer. Despite the danger coyotes posed for Marmalade on his nocturnal prowls, Lena did not object to their residency in the swamp beyond her bog; they did help, a little, to keep the deer population down. At one time in her life, in those heady days when she ate venison on a regular basis, Lena also did her part in reducing the deer population, by judicious use of her shotgun. Now as she entered her dotage, however, her heart had softened; she could no longer conceive, despite their depredations, of harming the graceful creatures.

Her softness of heart did not extend to Canada geese. Every year, just before Thanksgiving, she shot one (with her .22 rifle)—just one—to celebrate the season. (Despite initial misgivings, Cheryl had grown to appreciate the plump substitute for turkey, had even learned Lena's secret—stuffing the bird with pears, apples, onions, and other fruits and vegetables—for ridding the meat of some of its gamy flavor.)

Pesky fowls.

They did incalculable damage to the cranberry vines, blossoms, and ripening berries, trampling everything with their big, clumsy feet. (She was reminded of a favorite song by Fats Waller, "Your Feets Too Big.") Not to mention their excrement, great gobs of goose guano which littered the bog, the dikes, the shore.

She sighed. Of all things, letting her mind wander. From

poetry to excrement!

Oh well, just a symptom of cabin fever. It had been a long, hard winter.

Spring, or an approximation of it, would arrive in a week or two. In the meantime she needed a worthwhile project to occupy her mind. Maybe helping Frank with his current predicament? He had sounded worried over the phone—quite unlike him.

In the meantime, target practice—that might fit the bill. She was getting rusty, hadn't fired a weapon since last summer, when she had put her .22 pistol to good use dealing with a villain who threatened Marmalade. (She had not shot the man, exactly. She had just...well, best not to dwell on such things.) She thought, instead, of her arsenal. Besides the .22 pistol, she possessed the .22 rifle, bane of not only the Canada goose tribe but also of the muskrat clan (hadn't that trusty weapon come in handy on one or two occasions! Had saved her life, in fact) and of course her equally trusty double-barreled shotgun. That little baby was a formidable weapon. Not that she had blown any heads off with it—not yet.

Somehow her thoughts drifted from the shotgun to the bottle of wine that Frank was sure to bring with him this afternoon (not that she didn't have cases of it stashed away in a back room of her basement, stored on racks which she'd had installed especially for the purpose). They would have to enjoy the wine in the library, though. Too cold for the gazebo. Well, she would make the best of the situation by lighting a fire—Marmalade would want to warm his bones before it. Though still a young cat, he would soon be approaching middle age. She pictured him wearing bifocals...

My, her mind was not only drifting, it was being swept along by currents.

"An old vine zinfandel!" Lena carried the bottle into the kitchen, uncorked it, and returned with the bottle, and two crystal glasses, to the library where Frank—and Marmalade—had positioned themselves before the crackling fire.

"Fancy stemware," Frank said admiringly.

"A wedding gift," Lena said. "A set of four. Can you guess from who?"

Frank shook his head.

"Your father."

"Really?"

Lena nodded. "Rinaldo and I saved them for special occasions. And then, after he died, I put them away. Too painful a reminder, you see, of the happiness we shared. All too briefly, as you know."

"But now?"

"Oh, that was so long ago. Now that I'm on into my seventies I find comfort in things that remind me of him. I'm being a silly old woman, I guess."

"You're not old, Lena, and you know it. You're just looking for an excuse to drink more wine."

Lena laughed. "There's truth in that, I'll admit. Now, I'll pour us each a glass, and then you can fill me in on what's been going on."

Frank took a moment to appreciate the wine, one of the finer old vine zinfandels from a winery in Lodi, California. (Feeling guilty about burdening himself upon Lena, the least he could do, he felt, was select a decent wine as a gift.) He swirled it around in the crystal, sniffed it, and took a sip which he let linger in his mouth before swallowing. Only then did he speak.

"Detective 'call me Ben' Andrade is being very chummy, paying visits to my home almost daily—Laura suggests that we fix up the spare bedroom for him, to save him the bother of driving back and forth. 'Just one more question, Frank.' He insists on a first name basis, as if he and I are pals of long standing, and his visits are purely social. Or, 'Tell me again exactly why you chose that particular day to pay a call on Morales. Why was it, you said, that you didn't attempt to phone him first?'"

"On the surface it does look suspicious, Frank...your finding both bodies. Especially after Andrade—and I, just by happenstance—saw this Morales fellow scampering away from you in the parking lot."

Frank made a gesture with his hands: indicative of half agreement, half resignation. He didn't bother to point out that it was the sight of Detective Andrade that caused Pablo to do a bunk.

"But," Lena added, "closer examination of the circumstances should lower a reasonable person's level of suspicion."

"I'm not sure I follow."

"Well, at first glance your finding two dead bodies a few weeks apart seems like a coincidence. Too much of a coincidence, perhaps."

"That's what Andrade evidently thinks."

"But there are degrees of coincidence, Frank," Lena asseverated.

She held her wineglass up against the glow cast by the flickering flames, and admired the mellow shades of purple that danced within the crystal. "Oh, why do I love the juice of the grape so? You know, before I married an Italian I had never drunk wine. Not real wine, anyhow."

Patiently, Frank waited for Lena to return to the subject at hand.

"We don't have the faintest idea why Peter Gilbert was where he was when he died," she said at last. "BUT—capital letters, Frank—BUT you two had a prior connection; you knew one another. So he presumably had a purpose for coming to see you;

just because we don't know what that purpose is, doesn't mean it doesn't exist."

"I know, but—"

"Let me finish," Lena said, cutting him off mid sentence. "My point is, if Peter Gilbert had a purpose for visiting you that day, then your finding his body wasn't a true coincidence, in the way that it would have been, say, had you found him in some parking lot, or along the side of the road in some other town."

"I doubt whether such subtleties of ratiocination would impress my buddy Ben," Frank observed.

"They might a jury, though," Lena pointed out.

Frank threw his hands up in a gesture of mock despair. "Thanks, Lena, for cheering me up," he exclaimed. "So now you've gone a step further," he added in a more somber tone. "You've got me standing trial. For which murder? Both I presume."

"Now Frank. I haven't finished. Compose yourself. Take another sip of this excellent wine. See how easy it is; follow my example." She took a sip from her glass and swished it around inside her mouth. "Nectar of the gods."

"It is good wine, isn't it," Frank agreed. "I wonder if I can request it for my last meal."

"They don't have the death penalty in Massachusetts," Lena reminded him.

She took another swallow, then said: "Now let's get serious again. The fact that you found this Pablo's body is, again, not that great a coincidence. After all, he more or less requested a meeting with you. He lived alone, in a lonely spot. It's no great surprise that you were the one to find his body. Who else would have? This Juan Carlos you mentioned perhaps."

"Carlos Juan."

"Whatever. The point is you have nothing to worry about."

"Easy for you to say."

"I know. Which is why I'm going to get to the bottom of these two deaths."

Frank smiled. "Thanks, Lena." He took a deep breath, as if he were about to dive underwater, held it, then let it out slowly through his mouth. "Originally, before I found Pablo, I had intended to ask you to help me. But now, much as I appreciate your offer, no way am I going to allow you to get mixed up in this thing. That's not why I came here today. I came…well, I came because I needed a sympathetic listener. And as usual, you haven't disappointed me."

"Hogwash. I feel bad for your predicament, Frank, but my reasons for getting involved are, I must confess, not entirely unselfish. I need a project, something to give me purpose in life." Seeing he was about to protest she held up her hand. "No objections!"

Frank sighed. "You're the most obstinate woman I've ever known, Lena. Okay. Go ahead, snoop around. Not that you have a snowball's chance in hell of finding anything," he added.

"I'll ignore your vote of 'no confidence,' Frank," Lena said, with a smug smile.

Frank lowered his eyebrows and glared at her. "And just how am I to interpret that Marmalade look on your face?"

"'Marmalade look'? What on earth are you talking about?"

"That cat-that-ate-the-canary expression. Lena—is there something you know about all this that I don't?"

"What ever could I know that you don't, Frank?" she asked innocently. Then added, after an appropriate pause: "Other than a possible motive for both murders."

Frank made a guttural sound. "Methinks you've partaken too much of the grape."

Lena got up from her chair. "Keep an eye on the fire, will you, while I fetch something that I think might interest you."

Before leaving the room, however, she went over to the fireplace to stroke Marmalade, who was stretched out lengthwise before it, like a sated boa napping on a ledge.

"Just as I thought," Lena murmured. "His fur is so hot it's close to the ignition point. I don't see how he can stand it."

"It's nothing like the heat I'm beginning to feel," Frank quipped.

"Oh, come off it, Frank. Nobody, not even Detective Andrade, really thinks you murdered either of those men. He probably thinks you know more about their deaths than you're letting on, that's all."

With that she left the room.

Minutes later she returned with R. A.'s account of the Hickman secret clutched in her hand. "Here, take a gander at this." She dropped the four photocopied sheets onto his lap."

"What is it?" Frank asked, glancing at the topmost sheet.

"I'll explain after you've read it," Lena said. "Here's a tad more wine to sustain you in the meantime." She divided the remainder of the zinfandel in equal portions between their two glasses.

Ignoring his wine, Frank leaned into the light cast by the floor lamp that stood to the right of his chair and began to read. He read straight through, all four pages of handwritten script, without comment. When he finished he glanced toward Lena.

"Interesting."

"Is that all you have to say?"

"What else is there to say? It's a fascinating story, if it's true, which I seriously doubt. Where'd you get this?"

"Cheryl came across it, quite serendipitously, written in pencil on the flyleaf of a book on New England hauntings."

"A hoax, probably," Frank said. Remembering his wine, he took a sip.

"I don't think so, Frank," Lena asserted. She spoke with such fervor that a startled Marmalade lifted his head and turned an inquiring eye in her direction.

As if to emphasize her point she rose from her chair and began to pace up and down the room. "I think the Hickman treasure was real. I did some research at the Middleborough Public Library on Judge Peter Oliver. He was one of the most prominent and influential men in Massachusetts, highly esteemed for years, but in the end hated because of his loyalty to the king. It's an historical fact that his house—I should say his mansion—was ransacked, and burned, by an angry mob. Supposedly they were patriots, but I think some of them were there just for the looting. Jabez Hickman, for instance."

Frank shook his head. "All that may be true. Let's suppose this R. A. was telling the truth, and there was a Hickman treasure, and he did find a ring hidden in the old farmhouse. So what? What's it got to do with the deaths of Peter Gilbert and Pablo Morales?"

"Use your imagination, Frank," Lena said. She stopped pacing and returned to her chair. Noticing that a finger or two of wine remained in her glass she quaffed it.

"Cheryl thinks I'm becoming an alcoholic, Frank. What do you think?"

He laughed. "You're a bit too fond of wine, there's no denying that, but you know when to quit. No, you're not an alcoholic, Lena. Just a hopeless romantic. In the *Treasure Island* sense of the word."

"I take that as a compliment, Frank. There's a streak of pirate in me I'll admit. Now, getting down to brass tacks: Peter Gilbert and Beatrice Souza bought the old Hickman property, the part that remained after the outlying fields were set aside by the Town as conservation land. Drawing on his expertise as a landscaper, and possessing the equipment and men to do the job, Peter built a series of greenhouses for Beatrice, sheds for his own enterprise, and an office building which they shared.

"Here's what I think. I think Molly Hickman, realizing that she had revealed too much in her letters to her brother, fearing that knowledge of the family secret might fall into the wrong hands, removed whatever was left of the treasure from its hiding place in the kitchen and buried it somewhere outside. Do you follow, Frank?"

Frank chuckled. "You sound like a schoolmarm, Lena."

"Humph. Then act like teacher's pet and pay attention. But first, answer a question. In the old days, where did farmers hide their valuables in times of trouble?"

"Well, old Jabez hid his behind the kitchen cupboard."

Lena shook her head in exasperation. "That was different, Frank. That was a permanent hiding place. I mean, where did they hide their valuables temporarily, during the War of 1812 for instance, in case enemy soldiers ransacked the house?"

"Buried in the ground, I suppose. Maybe in the dirt cellar."

"In the ground, yes. Cellar, no—that's one of the first places marauders would look. More often than not, Frank, farmers— New England farmers especially—would bury their silver or whatever outside."

"Farms, even small farms, cover a lot of outside," Frank observed.

"Yes! You've just raised your grade from a C to a B, Frank. Because a farm could cover hundreds of acres, farmers had to bury their valuables in a spot they could easily remember."

"Like a well. Or maybe between the roots of a large elm or oak."

"Some actually did hide valuables in their wells," Lena conceded. "In a crevice in the lining, say. But wells were generally too risky. It's dangerous climbing in and out of a well; they're steep, narrow, and slippery. And if you inadvertently let something fall, it could stay submerged at the bottom for the rest of time.

"As for trees: over time (who knows how many years a war will last?) they risk being struck by lightning or otherwise destroyed. Besides, marauders might think to look there, too; there weren't that many trees on your typical Yankee farm. No Frank, not an ideal solution for hiding valuables."

She paused to catch her breath. "Stone walls, Frank. That was the hiding place of choice for your New England farmer of the eighteenth and nineteenth centuries. Along the base of a stone wall, in a spot easily remembered, and where there was no danger of the valuables being accidentally turned up by a plow."

Frank sat looking at his friend with amusement. "Quite the lecture, Lena. Where, pray tell, did you gain so much expertise on such an arcane subject?"

"Now Frank, don't make fun of me. I've been giving the matter a lot of thought."

She rose from her chair again, to the consternation of Marmalade, who was anxious for his tail—Lena, just a month or so ago, in the paroxysms of a heated discussion with Cheryl over the merits of red wine versus white, having accidentally planted her foot firmly upon it. Fortunately, the bloodcurdling yowl he let forth on the occasion was more one of outrage than of actual pain.

This time, however, rather than pace about Lena stood at the back of her chair and leaned upon it. Sighing, she said: "I know my theory sounds farfetched, Frank, but as I explained to Cheryl, I find it difficult to believe that two mysteries involving the Hickman place are not, no matter how obliquely, connected."

"What exactly is your theory?" Frank asked. "That Peter found the treasure, but refused to share it with Beatrice, so she killed him?"

"Something like that, I suppose. Or, knowing her character, he refused to hand over her share outright. Maybe, like the Hickmans, he was in favor of stashing it away for use sometime in the future. I haven't worked out all the details yet."

Frank got up. "I've got to shove off, Lena. But before I go, I have a theory of my own. Would you like to hear it?" Not waiting for her reply he went on: "My theory, like yours, is farfetched, but so far I haven't come up with anything better." He stooped to pat Marmalade. "Before she ruined her career by committing Medicaid fraud, Beatrice was a pharmacist. I don't think it's entirely without the realm of possibility…"

"My, Frank," Lena interjected, "you're beginning to sound like a schoolmarm, too."

Ignoring the interruption Frank continued: "…that Beatrice, with her knowledge of pharmaceuticals, has set up a meth lab somewhere on the property. Peter objected to it, threatened to, I don't know, tear it down—I don't think he'd actually have tipped off the police, he was too much in love with her to go that far. Anyhow, I think that's a more plausible explanation."

In the living room, as he donned his jacket, he said: "Lena, if you insist on snooping around—and for your own safety I wish you wouldn't—at least be very, very careful. I've already found two slabs of dead meat; I wouldn't want to find a third—especially yours. How would I ever explain that to Ben?"

CHAPTER XVII

Hollies and Gila Monsters

"What exactly are we looking for?" Cheryl asked.

"Anything that looks suspicious, dear."

"Like tomato plants camouflaged as roses?"

Lena favored her friend with a withering glance. "Don't be a wisenheimer." Making a show of examining the price tag attached to a potted azalea, she said, *sotto voce*: "We have two mysteries on our hands: a pair of murders that are obviously connected, and a treasure-trove gone missing. I'm convinced that the solution to both mysteries lies right here: the old Hickman place. We just have to dig around a bit."

"I hope you mean that figuratively," Cheryl said. She hefted a small China Boy holly in one hand, and a China Girl in the other.

"Why, of course I do," Lena assured her. Then, as an after-thought: "Although…"

"Now Lena, do you still have that bee in your bonnet?" Cheryl set the hollies to one side and glared at the older woman. "If you do, count me out. I'm not sneaking back here with pick and shovel some night when the moon is full to act like a gopher and dig up the place. Especially for a so-called treasure which I doubt exists, and if it does exist, has nothing to do with your two murders. One of which," she added, "may not even be murder."

"Can I help you find something?"

The person asking the question had entered the open-air shed devoted to evergreens without the two friends having noticed; screened by potted plants, she stood diagonally behind them, in an adjacent aisle.

Lena stiffened. How long had she been standing there?

She peered at the woman through a display of dwarf mountain laurels. As befitted her occupation the woman was, except for her boots, outfitted in forest green: heavy duty work shirt (festooned with stains of uncertain provenance), overalls to match. It was not surprising that neither Lena nor Cheryl had been aware of her presence; she blended right in with the evergreens, might have been one herself.

Where have I seen this medusa before? Lena asked herself.

You don't see a mug like that every day—or once having seen it, forget it. The woman might have been attractive once, before the sun took an ax to her and made her eyes all squinty, her brow furrowed, her nose wrinkled and hard, like a walnut. The sun's harsh rays had bleached her blonde hair with streaks of platinum, had baked her skin tough as leather. Her eyes, set narrowly apart, were reptilian—blue, but lizard-like.

She looked like something that had just crawled out of the desert.

The funeral home. That's where Lena had seen her before. In the front row, next to her doppelganger—someone who could have been her clone, had he not been male.

"I'm thinking about buying a holly bush for a friend," Cheryl said. "What's the difference between a China Boy and a China Girl?"

Before replying the woman glanced at Lena as if to say, *Is your friend for real?* "One's male, the other's female," she said to Cheryl. "You'll need both, if you want berries. We're running a

131

special. If you buy the Boy you get two Girls for the price of one."

"Sounds polygamous," Cheryl said, doubtfully. "I'll have to think about it."

With an air of *You're just wasting my time* the woman said, "If you make up your mind my brother or I will be glad to assist you. We'll be somewhere on the property." With a parting glance at Lena she left the shed.

"Now dear, don't overdo it," Lena admonished when the woman was out of sight. "Playing dumb is all well and good, but we don't want to call undue attention to ourselves."

"I couldn't help myself," Cheryl said. "I was curious to see whether the old Gila monster would give me a crash course on the birds and the bees." She paused. "Do you think she overheard anything?"

"I don't know," Lena replied. Then, using an old nautical expression that had still been current in her youth, added: "I don't like the cut of her jib."

They moved from the evergreens onto the pebble walkway that connected the various sheds and greenhouses making up the nursery. Although it was midweek, and still early in the season, they were not the only customers on the property. A dozen others were wandering about, some with stunned expressions on their faces, refugees in shock from the effects of the harsh winter, not totally convinced that spring had truly arrived.

"They're certainly sprucing up the place," Cheryl remarked as they strolled past a squat structure that had served as office for both Beatrice's nursery and Peter's landscaping business.

"The grieving Beatrice is wasting no time in erasing her lover's memory," Lena observed, nodding toward a carpenter who was removing the sign, nailed above the door, that had Peter's name on it. Close behind the carpenter a painter was smearing on white paint, so that no evidence of the sign would remain.

"Pentimento," Lena muttered.

"Pardon?"

"Oh, just talking to myself, dear. Seeing that worker paint over the discolored boards beneath where the sign used to hang reminds me of a poem I read the other day in *The Aurorean*, about March erasing winter—though traces of winter remain. I wonder if in years to come traces of Peter Gilbert will show through, as the paint fades."

"In the sense that 'Murder will out'?"

Lena smiled at her friend. "Very clever, dear." She nodded thoughtfully. "Yes, I believe that, with a little help from yours truly, justice will triumph. Murder will out."

As they rounded a bend in the walkway they were greeted by the rhythmic sounds of sawing and hammering.

"My," Lena remarked, "Beatrice certainly seems committed to rehabbing this place. Where's the money coming from? Insurance proceeds? Or has she located the Hickman treasure? Maybe she found it while Peter was still alive, and that's why she killed him."

"You're letting your imagination run riot again," Cheryl said. "You'd better not let anyone hear you; there are laws against slander."

"Pshaw. She's guilty as sin. Pablo Morales was on to her—that's why she killed him, before he had a chance to tell Frank what he knew."

Cheryl remained silent. Someone had killed the poor man, there was no arguing that.

They walked on until they came to a greenhouse with a sign in front that read *Vegetables*.

"Perhaps we should duck into here," Lena suggested. "I have more seedlings started in the sun room than I'll ever find room for in the garden, but I should buy something before we leave so as not to arouse suspicion. Perhaps a tray of lettuce."

"Don't bother," Cheryl said. "On the way out I plan to adopt."

"Adopt…?" Lena wrinkled her brow. "Oh, you mean the China Boy and China Girls. For a second you had me wondering. We could find space for a few more hollies I suppose. But you know, dear, the deer will only gobble them up next winter."

"They're not for us," Cheryl informed her. "They're a house-warming gift for a colleague at work who just bought a new house in Plympton."

"That's okay, then," Lena said, relieved. "I'm sure the deer in Plympton will appreciate them next winter when food is scarce."

They came to the end of the walkway. A wrought iron gate of modern design, filling the gap in a lichen-encrusted stone wall, blocked their way. A freshly painted sign attached to the gate read: *No entry beyond this point. Employees only!*

The gate was padlocked shut. Lena rattled it anyhow. Beyond the gate a paved roadway led first to several greenhouses, then curved from there out to the main road.

Lena nodded toward the gate. "That must have cost a pretty penny. And those greenhouses—they look brand new. I think I may just go take a peek."

"Lena! You'll get us thrown out. What part of *No entry beyond this point* don't you understand?"

"Nonsense. If anyone accosts me I'll pretend I'm just a confused old woman."

Exasperated, Cheryl quipped: "How about just a crazy old coot?"

Although the gate was nearly six feet tall, its purpose was purely symbolic; scarcely two feet in height, the stone wall, relic of the Hickman farm, proved no obstacle for a septuagenarian who had spent a good portion of her life romping over the New England countryside. It took Lena all of three seconds to boost herself over.

She stood and waited for Cheryl to follow.

"Well?" she demanded, when Cheryl failed to budge from her position on the other side.

"I am not going to trespass," Cheryl said through clenched teeth. "Certainly not on a wild goose chase."

"Don't mention wild geese, dear. The Canada geese have been especially bothersome this spring. They're pooping all over the place. It's as if they were constipated all winter and now the new shoots they're eating are acting like laxatives." She shook her head. "And their numbers keep growing. I may have to take drastic action this fall."

"Well, you may be a scofflaw," Cheryl said, "but I'm not. I'll wait for you by the evergreens."

"Now dear…"

The two friends were saved further argument by the arrival of a small van, which swung in from the main road and pulled to a stop next to Lena. A portly baldpate in his mid to late thirties—a Friar Tuck look-alike—got out of the vehicle and approached her.

"Good afternoon, ladies," he said affably, nodding first to Lena, then to Cheryl. "Is there anything I can help you with?"

"We were just admiring the way everything looks so inviting, so—so spic and span," Lena said.

"Why, thank you," the man said.

"What are those buildings over there?" Lena asked, pointing behind the man.

"As you can see we've expanded. Those're the greenhouses where we grow fresh herbs and veggies to sell to local restaurants."

"So that's why the public's not permitted?" Lena said, blithely ignoring the fact that she had already let herself into the forbidden zone.

The man nodded. "Almost everything we grow there you'll

find in the retail section. Now if you'll allow me to open the gate so that I can let you out…"

"Just one more question," Lena said. "We were so sorry to hear about poor Mr. Gilbert. He did some work for me many years ago—more years than I care to remember," she added with an embarrassed twitter. "A fine man. I was so saddened by his sudden passing that I attended his wake. What will happen to his landscaping business I wonder?"

"Well, Miss Souza has decided to discontinue it and concentrate solely on the nursery." He unlocked the gate and, in imitation of a grandee, bowed Lena out.

"It's been nice talking to you ladies. I'll tell you what—you've been so nice, when you decide to leave, be sure to stop at the register and tell them Joe Fairbanks said to give you a pot of daffodils. They're not in bloom yet but they will be shortly."

Before they had a chance to thank him he smiled and said: "Bye now, ladies." He closed the gate, snapped the lock shut, climbed into the van, and started the engine.

"Well now," Lena mused as Joe Fairbanks puttered off in the direction of the newly erected greenhouses. "A lot more pleasant than the Gila monster."

"A little too pleasant, don't you think?" Cheryl remarked.

"Ah, dear. You're beginning to think like a true detective. I wonder what else they're growing there, besides herbs and veggies. Frank thinks Beatrice may have set up a meth lab."

"I don't know—meth labs have a distinctive odor," Cheryl pointed out. "More likely a marijuana farm I'd guess."

"Hmm. I don't know about marijuana, dear—with so many states legalizing weed these days I don't see how there can be much of a future in it. But you may be right." She shrugged. "From what Frank Gallerani has told me about Beatrice Souza, and from what little I saw of her at the funeral home, I find it hard to believe that this operation is entirely aboveboard."

Cheryl glanced at her watch. "So what now, brown cow?" she asked. "I have a dinner date with Anthony this evening."

"Then let's get a move on," Lena said. "I think we've scouted out the place enough for today."

On the way to the checkout Cheryl stopped at the evergreens and selected two healthy-looking China Girls and a China Boy which, she hoped, would be equal to the task of keeping both ladies satisfied. As she paid for them at the register she said to the cashier—a male version of the blonde Gila monster—: "Mr. Fairbanks mentioned something about a pot of daffodils…"

Apparently taken aback he glanced up from the register. "Daffodils…oh yes. Of course." He scrutinized the two women closely. "Certainly. Compliments of the house. I happen to have a pot handy."

He groped down behind the counter. From his demeanor Lena half expected him to come up holding a sawed-off shotgun, or perhaps a live grenade. Instead the object he held in his hand was indeed a small pot of daffodils, their green spears bursting through the soil like the up-thrust beaks of baby birds imploring to be fed.

"Here you go. Do you need help getting these to your car?"

Cheryl shook her head. "No thank you, I'm sure we can manage." She handed the daffodils over to Lena, along with the China Boy, reserving the remaining two plants for herself to carry.

As they walked toward the parking area she said to Lena in a low voice: "I'm beginning to think you're right about this place. That bit about the daffodils—I think it was some sort of signal from Friar Tuck for the he-Gila monster to take a good look at us, for possible future reference."

"It's what I've been telling you all along, dear. There's something rotten in the state of Denmark."

CHAPTER XVIII
Lena Gears Up

Overnight, under a cloudless moonlit sky, the temperature dipped into the thirties on the uplands—even colder on the bogs.

That suited Lena Lombardi just fine; it gave her an excuse for bundling up. The deep pockets of her loose-fitting plaid jacket made the perfect place of concealment for, on the right, her trusty .22 pistol, together with an extra box of ammo—just in case; and on the left, for balance, a flashlight and a bundle of burglar tools—the latter on loan from Frank Gallerani. In the course of his work for the Bureau of Special Investigations for the Commonwealth of Massachusetts Frank had confiscated the tools from miscellaneous miscreants; finding the tools useful in helping to solve cases which required the occasional unlawful entry, he had neglected, whenever doing so would not jeopardize a conviction, to turn the tools over to the police.

"Don't tell me how you intend to use these," he said to Lena when she stopped by to borrow the tools.

"Don't worry, Frank," she reassured him. "We'll do this on a strictly need-to-know basis, just like they do in the CIA. If one of us is captured and tortured we won't be able to disclose what we don't know, will we. Have you ever been tortured, Frank?"

"No," Frank said, laughing. Then added: "Except by the women in my family. Especially my daughters—I'd rather have my teeth filed down by a mad dentist wielding a carpenter's rasp than be subjected, as I have been for hours, to some of the music Maria and Linda listen to on their devices."

"But you came close to being tortured once," Lena reminded him. "That time on the waterfront."

"Oh, you mean by Jack 'The Rat' Bartlett with his ice pick?" Frank nodded. "That was a close call I'll admit. If it hadn't been for Peter Gilbert…"

"Well, I can tell you this much, then," Lena said. "The tools are—indirectly—to avenge Peter Gilbert, if you get my drift."

Lena set her alarm for four a.m. Her bedroom was far enough away from Cheryl's for the noise of the alarm not to awaken her. Although her friend had assisted Lena in more than one caper of dubious legality, there was no need to involve Cheryl in this criminous venture.

The only task which Lena had to do this morning was to dress herself; the evening before she had showered before going to bed; earlier, while Cheryl was on her dinner date with Anthony she had tucked the pistol and flashlight and burglar tools into her jacket pockets.

What about breakfast? she asked herself as she laced her boots. She might have prepared something ahead of time, but hadn't given it a thought.

Just a quick bite, she decided. Toast and coffee. Well, maybe also an egg or two. She would scramble up a couple together with some American cheese, okay and some chopped onion, as soon as she fed Marmalade.

Speaking of whom…

As Lena crept down the stairs (taking care with each step not to cause the burglar tools to clink together), the orange tabby padded after her, slowly and deliberately, as if mocking her cautious gait. Though peeved at having been deprived, after a late evening's prowl, of a full night's sleep, he was reluctant to miss out on any comestibles (in addition to his customary breakfast) that chance might send his way.

"Stop your meowing," Lena scolded, when they reached the bottom of the staircase. "You'll wake Cheryl."

The cat sat on his haunches and gave her an injured look—his meows had been of the silent type—then, tail erect, scooted into the kitchen.

"None of your stinky food this morning—the smell might drift upstairs and awaken Cheryl and arouse her suspicion," she informed him, as he insinuated himself between her ankles. "You'll have to settle for chicken."

She fed him, then set about preparing breakfast.

By the time she was ready to leave, the predawn light had already brightened the east. She looked out the window with dismay; by rights, she should have arrived at her destination by now.

"That's what I get for dilly-dallying," she chided herself.

Perhaps she should abort the mission?

She mulled the matter over in her mind for a full three seconds before deciding upon an emphatic No!

Despite the extra hazards her dawdling had brought upon herself she would carry on.

Hastily, she scribbled a note for Cheryl: *Gone foraging.* (What Cheryl might make of the cryptic message was anybody's guess.) She left the note on the kitchen table, next to her friend's place mat. Without further ado she grabbed her jacket with its heavily laden pockets from the closet in which she had temporarily stored it, slipped into it—methodically, like a deep-sea diver of old donning a weighted-down suit with screw-on helmet to follow—gave Marmalade a parting pat on the head, and was out the door.

Which vehicle?

The pickup of course. This was no job for the sedan. She might encounter rough terrain.

The engine coughed into life. If the sound wakened Cheryl no matter; Lena was on her way.

CHAPTER XIX

On the Prowl

When, belatedly, she arrived at her destination she parked at the entrance to a recently constructed fire road. The road, little more than a crude lane designed to allow firefighting equipment access to brush fires, led through conservation land, property that had once been part of the old Hickman homestead. If she followed the road on foot it would, she hoped, lead her reasonably close to where she wanted to go, without having to tramp through swamps swollen by melted snow.

As soon as she swung off the paved road she realized that the pickup had been the right choice. Although its tires sank deep into waterlogged soil, she felt confident that when the time came—with rear tires spinning, spewing mud like water from a flushed hydrant—it would eventually return her to solid ground. Her sedan on the other hand would have become hopelessly mired. *At least I made one right decision this morning,* she congratulated herself.

She climbed down from the cab and immediately found herself ankle-deep in muck.

Damn!

Her boots, designed for bog work, were waterproof; even so the mud would slow her down—and she couldn't afford the delay. She needed to get a move on. It was light now; she was way behind schedule.

This is worse than wading through pig shit she grumbled as, laboriously, she lifted first one foot then the other, and painfully made her way toward firm ground. The effort reminded her of a bad dream she'd had the other night (brought on, conscience told her, by the injudicious uncorking of the evening's second bottle of Old Vine Zinfandel). In the nightmare she could see Marmalade, a long way off, being attacked by rabid coyotes. She tried to rush to his aid but her feet wouldn't budge; they felt as if they were weighted down by lead. She'd woken up panting and in a sweat.

She likewise found herself panting and, despite the cold, in a sweat when, at last, she came to the end of the mud patch and was able to stand on *terra firma*. "Get a grip on yourself, Lena," she muttered aloud. "You've still a long trek ahead."

A lifetime spent working on the cranberry bog that had been her parents' and then hers had left Lena in remarkably good shape for a woman now in her mid seventies, with few physical ailments other than the inevitable arthritis. Even so, she was no Wonder Woman.

She took a moment to catch her breath before setting off along the road into the woods. Though rough and uneven, especially where a bulldozer had gouged out and pushed aside stubborn stumps and boulders, the graveled surface was firm, walking not difficult. Trees and tall brush on each side shielded her from the breezes that ruffled their branches. The temperature had moderated since she left the house—the warming due, she realized, to the sun having prematurely mounted in the east. (*Prematurely*, she rebuked herself, because of her dalliance that morning.)

The fire road skirted a swamp that Lena recognized, by its rectangular shape and vestigial irrigation ditches, as the site of a long-abandoned cranberry bog.

O-ka-leee!

The cry, musical yet shrill, startled her: the first red-winged blackbird of the season. She spotted the male balanced on the tip of a cattail, flashing his brilliant red shoulder patches. The display was a warning to other males to piss off: this turf belonged to him. It was also, of course, an invitation for the ladies to come and check him out.

O-ka-leee!

The boisterous song cheered her, as did the bird's bold red chevrons—the color of ripe cranberries—as if the crops that failed to grow after the bog had been left to die had found an incarnation after all.

The delights of nature…all well and good, but she mustn't linger.

She forged on, like Dorothy in the Land of Oz, almost with a skipping motion—a manner of walking more suitable for a fifteen year old than a septuagenarian. The reason for this peculiar gait was the plaid jacket, with its weighted-down pockets, pulling her first to the left, then to the right, or so it seemed; not to mention her anxiety, the need to arrive at her destination in time to accomplish her mission.

The fire road cut through stone walls that had once separated fields, one from another, the fields now reverted to woodland. Someone, though, had done a yeoman's job of repairing the damage to the walls. Had the Town hired Peter Gilbert for the task? Lena recalled Frank's praise for the restoration work Gilbert did on Frank's stone wall.

The walls reminded Lena of her theory that Molly may have moved the Hickman treasure from the kitchen to the outdoors, and buried it at the base of a stone wall. Even if that supposition was true, seeing the extent of the walls made her realize the improbability of anyone ever finding the spot and, deliberately or accidentally, unearthing the treasure.

Then again…if Molly had relocated the treasure, she would have selected a location convenient to the house; the plot where the farmhouse had stood was now the center of Beatrice Souza's nursery—the site for which Peter Gilbert had done the preparation.

So, it was not inconceivable that…

Never mind the treasure. Concentrate on the task at hand.

Which wasn't being made easier by the fire road's sudden decision to loop away in a direction opposite to where she was headed. Well, that made sense, didn't it? The road was built to access the conservation land, not the nursery, which was already accessible by paved road.

Although Lena was not aware of it, she was tracing the last leg of the route which decades ago Ross Ashley had taken in pursuit of the Hickman treasure. Ashley, were he alive, would not recognize the terrain, so greatly had the generations-old farmland been altered by nature's reclamation. On his quixotic quest Ashley had, besides an impending nor'easter, the pitch black of night to contend with; on hers Lena had the density of lush, and occasionally hostile, vegetation.

She took a swig of water from a plastic bottle she'd slipped at the last minute into the pocket concealing the .22 pistol and soldiered on, the pale sun floating over the bare treetops like a poached egg.

The image reminded Lena of breakfast. What a fool I've been, she muttered to herself. Early start my ass. I'd have been better off starting later, sneaking in by means of the main entrance. What have I gained by coming in from the rear, other than the likelihood of contracting Lyme disease from the deer ticks I'm bound to pick up by the time I'm through?

Actually, in so much as she'd drenched herself in copious amounts of insect and tick repellent before leaving the house—so much so that Marmalade had retreated upstairs in order to avoid the reek—there was little probability that any but the most foolhardy of ticks would venture to crawl within ten yards of her.

If this was conservation land, open to the public, where were the walking trails? Not funded yet, probably. She made a resolution to volunteer her time, if not personally to hack away at the brush, at least to help raise money for the purpose.

She trudged on, through groves of new-growth cedar and pine, the immature trees alternating with brush rife with thorns, grape vines, bull briars, poison ivy: successors to the fields of corn and hay that for centuries had helped sustain, if only barely, the Hickman homestead. It was rough going. Though she considered herself a tough old buzzard Lena began to tire; her joints ached; her exposed flesh bore deep scratches from contact with the leafless vegetation.

I must look a fright, she chuckled to herself. If she were suddenly to meet up with the Gila monsters—the medusa and her male twin—and enter a beauty contest with them, Lena would, in her present state, come in third.

As fate would have it, it was neither the he- nor the she-Gila whom Lena first set eyes upon, but rather the baldpate, Joe Fairbanks, the portly pilgarlic whom Cheryl had dubbed Friar Tuck: Guardian of the Greenhouses. It was at the entrance to one of the *verboten* structures that she spotted him.

She crouched at the edge of the woods, shielding herself from view behind a trio of red cedars, in order to scope out the area. She found herself in a somewhat vulnerable position. A hundred yards separated her from the first of three greenhouses. The area in which the greenhouses stood was bounded off from the rest of the nursery by the stone wall with its wrought-iron gate. There were no other structures. Nothing but the three greenhouses, each with a propane tank attached, presumably to provide fuel for stoves to keep the plants within from freezing during frost.

There were no plantings in the intervening space, nothing save packed gravel buried under wood chips, and the paved roadway leading out to the main road.

Had her objective been sabotage, she could easily blow up the greenhouses by shooting at the propane tanks with her .22.

To reach the greenhouses she would have to scurry across the open space without cover. And yet, she asked herself, was not the risk of being seen minimal? Chances were, no one would notice her. But if by chance she was accosted, she could claim to have become lost in the woods while birding (and hope that no one questioned the absence of binoculars).

It was as she peered through the cedars (perhaps she should have brought binoculars along after all) contemplating her next move that Friar Tuck emerged out of the greenhouse nearest her. Like a woodchuck waking from a long winter's hibernation he pushed the door open, paused, yawned, scratched his belly, and slammed the door shut behind him with a backward thrust of his foot, before ambling off toward the wrought iron gate that led into the nursery proper. In no hurry to reach his destination, he paused halfway to scratch again, this time his crotch.

That had been a close call. Suppose she had ventured forth, and he had seen her.

Well, she hadn't, and he hadn't.

Shake a leg, fatso, Lena hissed. *I haven't got all day.*

He must have crabs, she thought, as he continued to scratch. Or else he's been in the woods to take a leak, and picked up a few ticks.

The itch alleviated, Joe Fairbanks moved on through the gate toward the shed that housed the evergreens. Lena waited until he rounded a bend before scooting toward the greenhouse he'd vacated. A lone crow, startled by the sudden movement, cawed raucously from the top branches of an ancient pine left over from the Hickman farm. Left standing by the Hickmans for the shade it provided livestock on broiling summer days, the pine offered the crow a convenient vantage point from which to spy on Lena.

Lena dashed across the open space and arrived at the door to the greenhouse confident that she had not been observed, other than by the irksome corvine. The bird kept up its cacophonous cawing, with the enthusiasm of a lookout in the employ of the nursery who had been promised extra pay for due diligence. Giving the bird a dirty backwards look, and a final shake of her fist—don't tempt me, don't tempt me, she muttered, patting the pocket that concealed the .22—Lena turned her attention to the door.

It was not locked. Only after she ducked inside and pulled the door shut did the thought occur that the walls of the greenhouse consisted of panes of glass. Moving about she would be clearly visible from the outside, perhaps not from a distance, but by anyone who chanced to pass by and glance within.

So what? To anyone who inquires I'm just browsing.

Not open to the public? Oh, I'm sorry, I didn't know.

Of course, that ruse would work only if she were wasting her time; that is to say, if the nursery was—in the argot of the underworld—*legit*. If on the other hand as Frank theorized, Beatrice and her cronies were operating a lab for the manufacture of methyl-amphetamine or, as Lena now suspected, a marijuana farm, discovery could prove more than just a little embarrassing. Drug lords—drug *lady* in the case of Beatrice?—don't take kindly to meddlesome old fogies.

No matter.

She once again patted the pocket wherein her pistol resided. She was prepared for any eventuality.

So this is how the expression "keeping a low profile" originated, she thought, as scrunching down, to the detriment of her spine and back muscles, she moved up and down the aisles, in a tolerable imitation of Groucho Marx, inspecting the plants. Obviously this was no meth lab; if such a thing existed on the property it would be housed in a regular building, not a glassed-in greenhouse.

And it was no marijuana farm.

It housed herbs. Herbs of all descriptions, herbs for all tastes. Dill, basil, rosemary, thyme. Bay leaf. Marjoram. Others which she did not recognize. She pinched two or three leaves at random. A rich aroma filled the air.

Fresh herbs for sale to local restaurants: this greenhouse was *legit*.

The fact that Joe Fairbanks AKA Friar Tuck had not locked the door when he left should have told her that there would be nothing incriminating inside. If she'd had her wits about her she could have saved herself time—and the misery of a sore back.

Lena slipped out the door. The crow had abandoned its post and was now quiet—amused perhaps by the antics of this strange old lady. She moved on to the next greenhouse. It's door, too, was unlocked. She poked her head in anyhow. More herbs.

Two down, one to go. If the third greenhouse turned out to be as herbaceously innocuous as the first two she would indeed have wasted her time. Without evidence of criminal activity, her investigation would not only stall, it would come to a grinding halt. The presence of Peter Gilbert's body on the road approaching Frank's house would never be explained. Worse, Frank would forever remain under a cloud of suspicion.

The third, and final, of the restricted-area greenhouses was set apart from the others. Was this a good sign? She estimated its distance from where she stood. Perhaps a hundred feet. She glanced around her. Her luck was holding; no one was about. She looked up at the sky—not in search of the upstart crow, whose existence she had already forgotten, but at the sun's position.

It was well after ten, she judged. The nursery would be open for business, the employees busy helping customers.

She hoped.

CHAPTER XX

Hue and Cry

The third greenhouse offered cause for hope. So preoccupied had Lena been with her reconnaissance of the first two that she did not notice till now that its glass panes had been painted black.

Could this be the meth lab?

She thought not. Though no expert on the manufacture and distribution of banned substances, she knew that the locations of meth labs were often betrayed by the telltale odors of the chemicals used in producing the drug. She sniffed the air; her keen nose detected no unusual odor, just the residue of the repellent she'd applied that morning, mingled with a trace of must.

Frank's speculation that Beatrice Souza was making and selling the stuff was just a wild guess.

What of her own (originally Cheryl's) equally wild guess: that Beatrice was raising marijuana as a cash crop? Didn't the plants require sunlight? Not much sunlight penetrated these blackened panes, that much was for certain.

And yet the door was padlocked. Why? The others weren't. Why this one?

She'd soon find out.

From her jacket pocket she extracted the burglar tools, neatly wrapped in a cloth bag, which she had on loan from Frank. Before handing the tools over he had given her a crash course on how to use them.

Sharp pains shot through her back as, bending, she spread the tools on the ground before her. An odd lot, they resembled a child's play set: miniature versions of tools a skilled workman might use in his trade: a short file; a jimmy with a claw on each end, one of them curved; a two-headed hammer, one head of steel, the other of hard rubber; a thin saw; a device for cutting glass; a suction cup; a roll of tape. Where was the tool she sought? "Ah, here's the little bugger!" She picked out a thin metal object that looked like a cross between a bobby pin and a skeleton key, and slipped the remaining tools into the bag.

Straightening, she waited for the pain in her back to subside, then inserted the tip of the device into the padlock. Gently, she jiggled it around the way Frank had showed her—as if cleaning her ear with a Q-tip—and *voilà!* in less than thirty seconds the lock popped open. She separated the padlock from the door and set it on the ground before reuniting the lock-pick with its companions in the bag, then returned the bag to her pocket.

She contemplated the door.

Suppose it was alarmed.

One way to find out. She grasped the handle and yanked the door open. Nothing. Unless it was a silent alarm, and somewhere lights were flashing. "You've been reading too many thrillers," she chided herself. Even so, she glanced about, to see if she could locate hidden cameras.

Satisfied that she was unobserved she stepped inside, but remained just within the doorway, to allow her eyes time to adjust to the dark. The musty smell she'd noticed before entering the greenhouse was more pronounced—a mixture of mold, it seemed, and something else, something faintly recognizable: moist sawdust. And horse manure?

Impatient with the time it was taking her eyes to adjust to

the gloom, she took out the flashlight and played its beam up and down the length of the greenhouse. Like the others, this one contained rows of wooden tables or platforms supporting plastic trays, crammed one up against the other. The trays were filled with some sort of brown soil-like mixture: judging from the odor, mostly composted sawdust and manure. She scraped a handful from the nearest tray and rubbed it between her fingers, then brought it to her nose. Sawdust and manure all right. Intermixed with what looked—and smelled like—shredded corncobs, along with various grains.

She groaned. The trays all contained the same crop.

Not herbs. Not cannabis.

Mushrooms.

Rows and rows of mushrooms. Tiny brown mushrooms. Exotic mushrooms with slender stalks and conical caps, similar to the mushrooms you find in Chinese dishes along with bamboo shoots, pea pods, water chestnuts, baby corn.

Legit.

Just another specialty crop intended for the local market.

Damn. She'd wasted her time after all—not that she minded, she had all the time in the world. But she'd given Frank false hope. She'd failed to come up with evidence that Beatrice Souza was in any way crooked: nothing to support Pablo Morales's claim that Beatrice was criminally responsible for Peter Gilbert's death.

All her fantasies about hidden treasure or illicit drugs. Just that: fantasies.

Fairy tales.

Fairy tales? *That's* what the mushrooms reminded her of— the inked images of brownies and gnomes the teacher used to rubber stamp on the children's wrists in grammar school when she was a little girl, as a reward whenever a child had performed exceptionally well. The mushroom caps were the same shape as the little caps the fairy-like creatures wore.

Fairy tales…

Something nagged at the back of her mind.

A faint hope—so faint that she was reluctant to voice it even to herself, lest it fade away the way the inked image on her wrist always faded away, when finally as a little girl she was compelled to wash her hands.

She set the flashlight on the edge of a table and took from her pocket the plastic storage bag she'd brought along with her in the hope—now forlorn—that she would need it to collect samples of marijuana plants as evidence.

She snapped the base of the stems of a half dozen mushrooms and dropped the caps into the bag. They felt slimy to the touch. Sealing the bag, she stuffed it into her pocket, along with the flashlight, and returned to the outside. There in the sunshine she stood and took deep breaths; after the mold- and manure-infused atmosphere of the greenhouse the fresh air tasted like chilled pinot gris.

An idea occurred: maybe her efforts this morning had not been wasted after all. Maybe she could find a use for all those great gobs of guano the Canada geese bestowed upon her bog with such largesse—as a substrate for growing mushrooms. She could convert part of her screenhouse, empty now save for the equipment stored there (and the ghost of the drowned Joe Baker) to cultivate a cash crop to make up for those years when cranberries failed or the market for them was poor.

She left off daydreaming and returned the padlock to its original position on the door and snapped it shut. There—no evidence of her ever having been here.

Now for the homeward trek.

"Hey! You!"

She spun around. No pesky crow this time sounding the alarm, but rather her old nemesis Joe Fairbanks, AKA Friar Tuck. He was through the gate, running toward her, moving quickly for a man of his corpulence.

He was not alone. The Gila twins—with their sun-bleached hair and green work outfits looking for all the world like angry ears of corn—were racing up from behind.

Had there been a silent alarm after all? Or was this just not her lucky day?

Did it matter which?

She set off for the woods.

Lena had never been a fast runner, not even in her youth. Now, hampered not only by arthritis but also by the bulky contents of her jacket pockets, she waddled more than ran—her progress not quite as slow as in her nightmare, yet not much faster.

She glanced behind. The trio were gaining.

Friar Tuck, puffing like a steam locomotive, was in the lead, the Gila twins close at his heels. In no great physical shape—heavy smokers in all probability—they too were gasping for breath. If she could reach the woods before they caught up with her she felt confident that she could elude capture.

If they did catch up with her, Lena had her pistol.

But could she justify using it? Or even brandishing it?

Massachusetts has strict gun laws. She didn't need a felony rap on her hands. Her pursuers were, after all, only doing their job. A bit too enthusiastically, perhaps. But well within their rights. It was she who was the intruder.

Just another twenty yards to go. She didn't dare lose momentum by pausing to glance rearward. By the sound of it, however, they were close upon her. She could hear, not only the crunch of three pairs of boots coming down hard on dry wood chips, but

Friar Tuck's stentorian gasps for breath as well.

A howl of pain followed by a shouted obscenity caused her to turn anyhow. Friar Tuck was down! He had tripped and lost his footing. As he attempted to lift himself from the ground the Gilas, unable to halt their own momentum, piled into him, landing on top, where they remained in a tangle of curses and flailing limbs.

Unable to restrain herself, Lena yelled "Whoopee!" and dashed into the woods.

CHAPTER XXI

Lena on the Lam

She plunged headlong into the line of brush that marked the boundary between nursery and conservation land.

Once inside the woods she had the advantage. The clowns on her tail weren't the type to spend their leisure time taking nature walks; they were not accustomed to moving through rough terrain. Baked by the sun to the consistency of cracked leather, the Gilas looked as though they had spent their working hours outdoors in the open, not in the woods. As for the portly pilgarlic, Joe Fairbanks, his wilderness ventures were limited to ambling along the landscaped walkway of the local McDonald's.

Feeling safe for the moment Lena slowed to catch her breath, and to take in her surroundings. Where the vegetation was sparse the as yet leafless growth offered scant cover—and her plaid jacket could hardly be classified as camouflage. Yet Lena knew that if she penetrated deep enough into the swamp before the stooges caught up with her she could easily elude them by concealing herself behind a clump of tussocks, or in a hollow, or submerged in water dyed brown by tannins, or by lying flat on her belly behind a fallen log or whatever evergreens—holly, cedar, hemlock, laurel—might offer themselves.

She figured, however, that she would have no need to retreat into the heart of the swamp—that her pursuers, having gone through the motions of giving chase, would soon give up. After all, they didn't strike her as paladins of private property, guardians of the gates, intolerant of even the slightest trespass, or self-righteous vigilantes. They had menial duties to perform back at the nursery; running after a prying old lady in order to scare her off—even if she had dared breach the boundaries of their precious domain—hardly seemed a likely priority.

Unless…

Unless they had something to hide. Something so vital to their self-interests that it was worth risking life and limb—theirs, as well as hers—to prevent its discovery. Perhaps their intent in giving pursuit was not to scare Lena off. Perhaps it was to silence her—permanently—the way someone had silenced Pablo Morales.

She gave the pistol in her pocket a reassuring pat.

If they intended her harm, she was ready.

She had killed before in self-defense. She could kill again.

She stood within a thick grove of pine saplings and listened. At first the only sounds she heard were the boisterous chirps of the mixed flock of chickadees, titmice, and white-breasted nuthatches whom she'd dislodged from their perches in the pines. Gracious about the eviction—not setting up a loud clamor the way their distant relative the crow had—they would soon quiet down, and not betray her position to the enemy.

As if the enemy could hear anything with the clamor they themselves were making.

The threesome were not far behind. Lena could not see her pursuers. But she could hear them shouting, cursing one another for their clumsiness, at the same time urging each other on.

She left the pine grove and quickened her pace.

On the way in that morning, once having left the fire road she had kept as much as possible to open spaces. Now she did the opposite, seeking out the densest brush, even though it made the going difficult as well as painful. Once she arrived home and showered—and checked for ticks—she would have to tend to her many wounds: superficial scratches for the most part, but a few more serious, requiring bandages.

The thought that her pursuers were bound to emerge from the woods in even worse condition cheered her. Crashing blindly through the underbrush like enraged rhinos, they would subject their exposed flesh—even the sun-cured hide of the Gila twins— to deep lacerations, from briars and the sharp tips of branches. They would bathe themselves in the sap of poison ivy, poison sumac, poison oak. They would be lucky not to break a leg, or poke an eye out.

Picking her way through a tangle of bull briars and poison ivy (she knew how to avoid contact with the venomous plant) Lena came to a sudden depression—an area of several hundred square feet that sloped gently down to end abruptly at a depth of about five feet, the whole enclosed and buttressed by a rectangular stone wall. An opening in the wall at the top of the depression had once been blocked by a sturdy wooden gate, now rotted to near nothingness.

Although vegetation had taken over the enclosed space, as it had everywhere else on the fields of the abandoned Hickman farm, the structure might once have been a redoubt or miniature fortress, a defense against Indian attack or against the Redcoats during the American Revolution. It was no such thing of course. Lena recognized it for what it actually was: a paddock, or more properly a pound, for the confinement of livestock—sheep, perhaps, ready for shearing.

She made a detour around the pound, still keeping in the general direction of the spot where she knew she would soon link up with the fire road. By now every bone in her body ached and she was dog-tired. She took a last swig from the plastic bottle—she had consumed most of the water on the way in. But at least she could now take her time. It had been a while since she'd last detected sounds of pursuit—no doubt the trio, abandoning as hopeless the attempt to apprehend—or eliminate—her, had turned back toward the nursery. The only danger was that, in typical stooge fashion, they might become lost and somehow circle back and blunder into her.

That was hardly likely though.

Having traveled little more than a dozen yards beyond the pound, in hopes of finding a path or a least an animal trail where the going would be easier, Lena stepped onto a small area strangely lacking in vegetation. Suddenly the ground let loose beneath her. In the time it takes to say, "Oh Shit!" she plummeted, feet-first, like Alice down the rabbit hole.

CHAPTER XXII

Holed Up

All was still, except for a centipede which strolled across the bridge of Lena's nose, and dangerously close to her eyes. The creature's tiny legs irritated her skin. Helpless to expel it, she snorted, to discourage it from attempting even more intimate explorations. Did the centipede have a destination in mind, or was it merely on walkabout? With luck it would not invade an ear.

Dust particles invaded her nostrils, causing her to sneeze; in the confined area the sound of the sneeze was what she imagined a dinosaur's fart might sound like. The force of the sneeze catapulted the centipede like a circus clown shot from a cannon.

Debris—remnants of the rotted boards that had given way under her weight, and the thin layer of soil and decayed vegetation that, accumulating over the years, had hidden the boards from sight—drifted onto Lena's hair and into her eyes. Or would have drifted into her eyes, had she not kept them tightly shut.

After a while she opened them.

Dazed, she found herself standing upright in a narrow hole. Tilting her head upward she saw, through the nimbus of floating dust, a perfectly round patch of blue sky.

As the shock brought on by her precipitous descent and its aftermath wore off she realized that she had fallen into an abandoned well. The well's proximity to the pound suggested that its purpose had been to supply water for the confined animals.

Gingerly, she tested first her left foot, then her right. No broken bones.

Two factors had saved her from serious injury. At some time the well had been used as a refuse dump; consequently it had been partially filled. Lena's under-footing consisted of a heap of rubble; the top of her head was only about five feet below ground level. And the well was narrow. Her jacket, with its bulky pockets, by scraping against the sides of the well after she dropped through the opening had helped cushion her fall.

The man who dug the well and lined it with stones must have been on the thin side. Downright skinny. Perhaps he had a tapeworm. Tapeworms were quite common in those days. Lena had read somewhere that in the present day there were obese individuals who deliberately ingested tapeworms in order to lose weight. The thought of swallowing a tapeworm caused her to gag.

The narrowness of the well, unfortunately, also hindered further movement.

She was by no means wedged tight, but her ability to adjust the position of her arms was limited.

She began to panic—the thought of dying like a spelunker trapped in a subterranean cavern did not appeal to her—but she found that by pressing her back hard against the stone lining of the well, twisting her body, and bending an elbow close to her, she was able to straighten her arm and raise it above her head. How doing so could help her out of her current predicament she didn't know, but the fact that she could raise her arm cheered her.

Less cheering was the realization that no one knew her whereabouts. The note she'd left next to Cheryl's place mat simply said "Gone foraging." Foraging for what, or where, Lena had purposely neglected to say.

Foraging for trouble? Foraging for death?

After years of resistance, Lena had finally been persuaded by Cheryl to acquire a cell phone. At the moment, the phone rested safe and secure in the glove compartment of her pickup.

The pickup! She'd left it at the entrance to the fire road. At some point it would be noticed. When Lena failed to return home that evening Cheryl would naturally become concerned, and eventually alarmed. Sooner or later she would notify the police. They would send out a Silver Alert. At some point the connection would be made between the pickup by the side of the road and the missing senior citizen.

A search of the woods would be made. Perhaps the searchers would find her, perhaps not. Even if they did find her, by then she'd probably be dead, from thirst or hypothermia.

Or should that be *hyper*thermia?

Hypothermia or hyperthermia. What difference does it make, if you're dead?

She had her pistol and plenty of ammo. She could fire shots into the air to attract attention. What the effect of firing a .22 pistol in such a confined area would have on her eardrums—all she had to go by was the evidence of the sneeze—she didn't care to contemplate. All in all, though, it was probably not a good idea—unless as a last resort.

If she was to get out of the well alive and unscathed she'd have to do it on her own, and quickly.

Perhaps she could claw her way up, like Spider Man—or, in her case, Crab Woman. She probed the well's lining with her fingers. It had been constructed using rough stones of various sizes, resulting in plenty of crevices between the stones.

She managed to get both arms upright and high in the air—like a revivalist in the throes of religious fervor shouting "Hallelujah" in praise of the Lord—then groped around for suitable finger holds. Although the well had gone dry sometime in the nineteenth century, moisture seeped through the porous soil from above, dampening the stones that lined the wall, making them slippery.

She located fingerholds for both hands and attempted to pull herself up. Forty years ago she might have been able to do so, but at her present age she found that, without proper leverage, she didn't have the strength. She tried anyhow, several times—straining, lifting herself off the rubble pile an inch or two only to lose her grip and fall back—until she'd ripped her nails and bloodied her hands.

She took a moment to rest.

Her arms ached, from her exertions and from holding them upright for so long. She felt like a victim of the Inquisition, first stretched on the rack then suspended from a dungeon wall. All she needed to complete the image were a rat or two to nibble at her toes.

How much longer would her arms be of any use to her? If I don't get out of here soon I never will, she thought.

Maybe I'm going about it backwards. Maybe I should begin with my feet.

She probed with her boot for a toehold. Finding one, three or four inches from the top of the rubble heap, she inserted the tip of the boot and pressed down, hard, as if kick-starting a bike. As she launched her body upward she grabbed for a crevice with her fingers, and for another toehold with her other boot.

The first time she failed to hold on. But on her second attempt she succeeded.

Hallelujah!

Praise the Lord indeed. So what had she gained? Possibly three inches.

The next step would be even harder. She no longer stood on solid footing, but clung precariously to the side of the well. A false move, a missed finger- or toehold, would send her slipping and sliding back to the bottom.

She'd have to take extreme care.

Better yet…

The burglar tools…why hadn't she thought of them sooner? Surely she could make use of at least one or two. But how to access the tools?

Simple. She would use the narrow confines of the well to her advantage. She leaned her back against the wall, like a loafer preparing to light a cigarette, while stretching a leg forward against the opposite side. Thus propped, she was able to fumble with her hand inside the pocket containing the bundle and slip the tools, still wrapped, onto her lap. Careful not to spill any, she felt around to see which of them might be of use.

Why of course! The bar with a claw at each end. The curved claw would serve her nicely. No longer did she have to depend on her torn and bloody fingers to maintain a hold in the crevices. The steel claw would dig in and hold on for her.

Captain Hook, eat your heart out, she murmured as she raised the steel claw and dug it into the well wall. With its firm grip she was able to pull herself higher, find toeholds for her feet, repeat the action, and slowly, ever so slowly, make her way toward the top.

The last eight or nine inches proved the hardest. She reached the point where she could actually raise her arm, with the claw, above the rim. But above the rim there was nothing for the claw to latch upon, other than air. With her free hand clutching the rim, she tossed the claw onto the surface, then by sheer force of will pulled herself with both hands over the edge of the well, where she lay, panting, on the sodden soil.

She lay belly down, too tired to roll over. Only when the chill began to seep through her clothing did she get up from the ground and move away from the site of her ordeal. She found a copse where she sank onto the leaf mold, and sat there, listening. There were no sounds; even the birds were silent. Taking no chances, she removed the .22 from her pocket and placed it in her lap. She almost hoped that one of her pursuers would find her; at that moment it would have given her great pleasure to shoot one of those responsible, albeit indirectly, for her plunge into the abyss.

When she had sufficiently recovered she brushed herself off as best she could and set off in the direction that would take her to the fire road.

CHAPTER XXIII
Bandages and Badinage

When Lena trudged through the doorway of her Greek Revival home Marmalade was right there on the rug to greet her.

"Marmalade, you don't know how glad I am to be home!" she exclaimed.

The cat took one look at her, flattened his ears, and with bristled fur darted from the room.

"Marmalade!" Lena shouted after him. "Don't pretend you don't recognize me. I'm not *that* much of a mess."

Reassured by the familiar voice, and mindful that it was past his feeding time (Marmalade enjoyed three squares a day, plus the occasional snack) he plodded back into the room, tail erect, as if nothing untoward had happened.

Although she had left the house a lifetime ago, it seemed, the clock in the kitchen told Lena that it was only ten past two. She would have plenty of time to swallow a handful of aspirins, shower, change her clothes, and apply ointments and bandages to her wounds, before Cheryl returned home from Bridgewater State University.

Lena's first task, however, after scooping food into Marmalade's dish, was to phone Anthony.

Even though Anthony Gomes had been Cheryl's "significant

other" for several years now, Lena had never had occasion to call him at his job in the laboratory at Ocean Spray's cooperate headquarters in Lakeville, where he was employed as a research scientist. However, as a member of the Cranberry Growers' Association she had the main number readily at hand.

"Lena!" Anthony exclaimed when she was finally put through.

"I hope you don't mind my calling you at work."

"Not at all. Uh, is anything wrong?"

"Everything's fine," Lena assured him. "Look, Anthony, I'm calling to ask a favor."

"Certainly," he said, though she could hear the puzzlement in his voice. "What can I do to help you, Lena?" He paused. "Does it concern Cheryl?"

"Nothing to do with Cheryl." It was her turn to pause. "Would you mind dropping by after work? I know it's out of your way…"

"Not all that much out of my way," Anthony said cheerfully. "A few miles at most. It's not as though it will be the first time I will have driven there after work," he reminded her.

"Good. That's settled then."

"Are you going to tell me what this is all about? You've piqued my curiosity."

"I'd rather not say over the phone," Lena told him. "It's really just a small favor. You can stay for supper if you like. I hope you don't mind, it'll be pot luck."

"Thanks anyhow, Lena, but not this evening. My sister Irene is making her special jag and would be hurt if I passed it up. I'll phone her and Ma and tell them I'll be a little late. They won't mind."

"You'll at least have a glass of wine with us? Cheryl should be home by then."

"You've twisted my arm. Wine sounds great. I've gotta go

now, Lena. See you after work."

As a professor of English Literature at Bridgewater State University, Cheryl Fernandes sometimes arrived home in the early afternoon, sometimes late in the evening, the length of her workday dictated not only by a classroom schedule that varied from day to day, but also by scheduled and unscheduled appointments with students, faculty meetings, school functions, and her own research at the library. Although she tried to let Lena know in advance the approximate time of her return, that was not always possible.

The two women enjoyed sharing meals together. Both excellent cooks, they enjoyed preparing meals for one another, and for Marmalade, who although he tolerated canned cat food (of gourmet quality), preferred his seafood fresh from the pan or oven.

As predicted, Cheryl arrived before Anthony.

When she walked into the kitchen, where she knew she would find Lena, her reaction upon seeing her friend was much the same as Marmalade's had been, although unlike the cat she refrained from flattening her ears and darting out of the room.

"Lena! Wherever did you go foraging? The Amazon River basin? Were you mauled by a jaguar?"

"You're being a wisenheimer again, dear," Lena replied, without looking up from the chopping board where she was busily dicing celery as an ingredient for shrimp salad canapés, one of the hors d'oeuvres she would offer Anthony. "First Marmalade, now you."

"Well, you do look like you've had an altercation with a grizzly bear, the latter being the victor. Where exactly have you been?"

"I'll tell you later, dear, after Anthony leaves."

"Anthony? Is he here?"

"No, but I'm expecting him shortly."

"For supper?"

Lena shook her head. "For wine and hors d'oeuvres."

Cheryl knew from past experience that for the present she would get no further information from Lena. "I'd better go up and change," she said. "Where's Marmalade?"

"Roaming the wilderness. He kept pestering me, so I stuffed him with shrimp and shoved him out the door."

Anthony arrived fifteen minutes later. Cheryl greeted him at the door with a hug and a kiss, and said: "Lena's acting very mysterious. She won't tell me why she asked you over."

"She wouldn't tell me either," Anthony said, as he followed Cheryl into the library. "Except to say that she needs a small favor from me."

Before Cheryl could comment Lena called from the kitchen. "Can you give me a hand, dear? Fetch this tray of hors d'oeuvres while I open the wine." To Anthony, she shouted: "Pinot gris?"

"What year?" Anthony shouted back.

"Don't be a wisenheimer like your girlfriend," Lena hollered. "First Marmalade. Then Cheryl. Now you."

"Whatever is she talking about?" he asked Cheryl.

Cheryl laughed. "Wait till you see her." With that she left the library for the kitchen.

She reentered moments later with the hors d'oeuvres, with

Lena close on her heels, carrying a tray with the wine and glasses.

Having been duly warned, Anthony did not comment on the bandages and ointment, merely rose from his chair and gave her a peck on the cheek.

As they sat sipping wine and munching on canapés, he said: "Now what is it I can do for you, Lena?"

"Just a minute," she said. She left the library and returned to the kitchen. When she came back she held a small freezer bag in her hand.

"I found these today," she said to Anthony, handing him the bag with its contents.

He looked inside and examined the three mushrooms. "Ah," he joked. "More hors d'oeuvres. I'm sorry, Lena, but I'll have to pass. I want to save room for Irene's jag."

"Seriously, Anthony, I'd like you to identify these for me."

He studied them again. "I think I know what they are, but I can't be sure. Okay if I bring them back to the lab tomorrow and look at them more scientifically?"

"I was hoping you'd say that," Lena said.

"May I ask where you got them?"

"I'd rather not say for now," Lena replied. "Not until you've positively identified them."

"I should have an answer for you tomorrow morning, at the latest."

"I knew I could count on you," Lena said. "More wine?"

After Anthony had departed for home and his sister's jag, Lena said to Cheryl: "There's an identical bag of mushrooms in the refrigerator, dear. Be sure not to eat them. There's someone else I want to show them to."

CHAPTER XXIV
The Magic Revealed

"Ah, Detective Andrade, so good of you to accept Frank's invitation," Lena said to the policeman, who upon her entrance into the room graciously relinquished his seat next to the Franklin stove so that she could take advantage of its warmth. Although the calendar stated that spring had arrived, the New England climate insisted that it hadn't, not quite. A chill wind gusted from the north, tossing the heads of daffodils to and fro, like so many saucy wenches.

"I'm Lena Lombardi, a good friend of Frank's. This meeting was my idea."

"We've met," he remarked.

"Yes, at Peter Gilbert's wake. I introduced myself, but you seemed distracted at the time."

"For which I apologize," he said, though by his demeanor he appeared anything but contrite. Truth be told, the Rochester detective was annoyed by the last-minute phone call he'd received from Frank Gallerani, informing him that Frank's friend, Lena Lombardi, requested his presence at a meeting during which, she claimed, she would reveal not only the motive for Peter Gilbert's murder, but also the method by which it had been carried out.

"Motive and method are one and the same," Lena explained, as, after preliminaries, the three—Frank, Andrade, and Lena—

sat in the parlor overlooking Frank's cranberry bog sipping the strong, bitter coffee Frank had brewed for the occasion.

Neither of the men seemed to notice Lena's many bruises and abrasions. They were too much the gentlemen to comment on a lady's appearance.

"Method first, if you will, Mrs. Lombardi," Andrade said, in the tone of one who, though bound by the strictures of professional courtesy, is convinced that his time is being grievously wasted.

"Well, in a nutshell, Peter Gilbert was murdered by magic," Lena said.

The silence following her pronouncement was palpable. Frank, in whom Lena had so far confided nothing, but who had agreed through faith in his eccentric friend's soundness of mind to host this impromptu meeting, attempted, visibly, to shrink himself into nothingness; whereas on his part, Detective Andrade, accustomed as he was to dealing with kooks, cranks, and crackpots of all stripes, merely tapped his long fingertips against the side of his coffee mug, with only the slightest moue of disdain marring his otherwise impassive countenance.

"Not invisible magic, mind you," Lena said, secretly enjoying her audience's discomfort. "No abracadabra stuff. Tangible magic." Reaching into a cloth clutch—such a nice floral pattern, white and red roses, so appropriate for the occasion—which upon sitting down she had unobtrusively placed by her feet, she extracted a plastic freezer bag. The bag and its contents were identical to the one which two days previously she had handed over to Anthony.

This one she handed to Detective Andrade.

Frank, who had caught a glimpse of the bag's contents as it passed by his face, said: "Mushrooms?"

"I'm afraid they're a bit mushy. I picked them two days ago

and was, how shall I put it? delayed in getting them home."

Lena could tell from Frank's expression that his faith in her, though not yet completely restored, was beginning to reassert itself. Perhaps, he was probably thinking, his eccentric friend wasn't completely balmy after all.

Meanwhile Andrade, who without removing them from the bag had studied the mushrooms closely, said: "Are they poisonous?" Then, not waiting for an answer, added: "Even if they are, I don't see what possible relevance they can have to Peter Gilbert's death, or his presence on this property."

"Not poisonous. Not exactly," Lena said. "Their scientific name is *Psilocybe semilanceata*. Otherwise known as Liberty Cap mushrooms, because of the shape of the caps—similar to the caps worn by Parisians during the French Revolution. I personally think they resemble the little hats worn by fairies, but who am I to say?"

"Liberty Cap mushrooms?" Andrade said. "If they are Liberty Caps, they're a controlled substance. A Class C substance, to be exact. Possession of which, I believe I need not point out, is a serious offense in Massachusetts."

"Oh, don't worry, we won't tell on you, Detective Andrade, will we Frank?" Lena joked. Seeing Andrade's blank stare she added, "Well, at this moment it is you—not I—who has possession of them."

Losing patience, an exasperated Andrade said, "Mrs. Lombardi, where did you get these?"

"I told you, Ben. May I call you Ben? You don't object?" Lena knew how to rattle the detective's cage, and was enjoying herself immensely. "I picked them two days ago."

"As I'm sure you know perfectly well, Mrs. Lombardi, Liberty Cap mushrooms are not native to this area."

"No, they're not," Lena agreed. "They're native to the Pacific

Northwest—especially common on the Oregon coast I'm told. Also found in Quebec, I believe."

"Do you mind if I stick in my oar?" Frank asked. "They're hallucinogenic, right?"

Andrade nodded. "They've been used for thousands of years by Native Americans in their rituals. Still are, in fact. The effects of ingesting the mushroom are similar to those induced by LSD." He paused, and looked at Lena. "They're also commonly called Magic Mushrooms, for the effects they have on people. In the Middle Ages, witches in Europe used them to induce psychic states."

"Now Ben, you're not implying that I'm a witch, are you?" Lena asked, innocently.

"Actually," the detective responded, "I'm beginning to get an inkling of what you're implying."

"Which is, I believe," Frank interjected, "that Peter Gilbert may have been under the influence of the drug when he wandered onto my property."

Lena nodded. "Now that you both see my drift—my, all these nautical expressions!—I'll come clean and tell the whole story. I found these growing in a greenhouse in Beatrice Souza's nursery."

She related the whole of her escapade at the nursery, not omitting the part about falling into the abandoned well. "Something should be done about covering that well, or filling it in; someone else might fall into it, and not be so lucky as I was in getting out." She then went on to explain that she consulted a friend of hers—not to be named—who conducted tests and confirmed the mushroom's identity. "Hence my presence here today," she concluded.

Andrade remained silent.

Frank said, "But there's more, isn't there, Lena? You promised proof of motive as well as method."

"*Au contraire, mon cher*," Lena said. Then: "Hey, that rhymes! I'm a poet and don't know it."

"But your feet show it," Frank said. "They're Longfellows."

"When you two are finished…" Andrade said. However his manner, Lena noted, was now almost cordial, compared to what it had been.

"Anyhow, I never said anything about proof," Lena resumed. "It's pure speculation—although I'm pretty positive that my supposition is correct."

"Which is…"

She turned to the detective. "From what Frank has told me about Peter Gilbert, I believe the man didn't have a crooked bone in his body. It was his misfortune, however, to fall—and remain—hopelessly in love with Beatrice Souza, who is anything but honest."

"She's probably a sociopath," Frank commented. "Without conscience."

Lena nodded. "What I think happened is, Peter somehow discovered Beatrice's illicit operation." She shrugged. "Maybe it was Pablo Morales who discovered the mushrooms, and then told Peter. In any case Peter threatened to—I don't know exactly what. I don't think he would have reported the woman he loved to the police. But he probably threatened to destroy the mushrooms, and prevent her from starting up again in the future.

"If ever Beatrice loved Peter—which I seriously doubt, I think she just used him—she no longer did. He was a threat to her ill-gotten gains; she needed to get rid of him. What better way, than to feed him the drug—the autopsy report, remember, said that Peter's last meal consisted of an omelet made, in part, with *mushrooms*…Where was I? Oh…to feed him the drug on a day on which she knew he would venture out on roads made extremely hazardous by ice and snow. And sure enough, under the effects of the drug he did spin off the road. He wasn't killed outright, but we know the rest."

"In his disoriented state he wandered off," Andrade said. "And ended up here."

"Exactly," Lena said.

"But we have no proof that any of this actually happened," Frank pointed out. "Even if I'm in the clear—" he glanced at Andrade, who nodded in affirmation— "it looks as though Beatrice will get off scot free."

"Not necessarily," Andrade said. "There's something I haven't told you. Normally I wouldn't tell you, but under the circumstances…you've certainly helped clear matters up, Mrs. Lombardi…I think it's safe to confide in you. I'm about to arrest Beatrice Souza for the murder of Pablo Morales."

"You have proof?" Lena asked.

"Forensic evidence," Andrade replied. "I won't go into the details of what we found—the prosecutors will do that in court—but we can definitely prove that Beatrice was at one time in Morales's apartment. We also have witnesses—Morales's neighbors—who saw her drive in, then out, around the estimated time of death. Until today I didn't think we had much of a case. But now that you've provided me with a possible motive—to keep Morales quiet about the Magic Mushrooms, and maybe in revenge for his informing Peter—I think we can move forward.

"We can certainly charge her, thanks to you, Mrs. Lombardi, with trafficking in an illegal substance." He handed her the freezer bag with the mushrooms still inside. "You'd better dispose of this."

"But won't you need it for evidence?"

Andrade shook his head. "It was illegally obtained. Useless to us. But," he added with a smile, "now that we know it exists, and where to find it, we can, shall I say, stumble upon it while executing a search warrant of the nursery, based on probable cause on suspicion of murder."

CHAPTER XXV

The Secret Exposed

Frank stood at the window and watched as Andrade's unmarked police cruiser bumped along the dirt track that led from the house, by the bog, through the swamp, and out onto the paved road.

"You know, I'm beginning to like 'Ben,'" he said to Lena, who stood beside him, coffee mug in hand.

"Now that he no longer thinks you're guilty, or withholding information."

"I have you to thank for that. Here," he said, taking the mug from her, "let me replace this with a glass of pinot noir. I would have offered wine instead of coffee earlier, but I figured Andrade wouldn't want to drink while on duty."

Lena surprised Frank by shaking her head. "No wine for me at the moment, thank you."

"Lena! Are you ill?"

"What's it with these wisenheimers?" Lena asked aloud, to herself and to the room.

"Wisenheimers?"

"A private joke, Frank."

"I prefer 'wiseacre' myself. Or just plain 'wise guy.' Seriously, no wine?"

Lena shook her head. "Perhaps later. First, though, can we

take a stroll outside?"

"Of course. But if it's just to rid yourself of those Magic Mushrooms, I can toss them into the compost bucket under the kitchen sink. I empty it into the compost pile behind the house every evening. The raccoons that make their rounds and rummage through the pile every night are entitled to a psychedelic trip now and then."

Lena handed over the freezer bag. "To tell the truth, I'd forgotten all about the mushrooms. But I'd still like to go for that stroll."

Anthropologists studying the customs and mores of Cape Cod cranberry growers would have recognized as typical behavior the stance that Frank and Lena took once they had reached the outdoors: standing on shore and gazing out over the wide expanse of newly exposed vines, burgundy-hued after a long winter's sleep beneath ice and snow. The two might have been mariners mesmerized by the vastness of the sea—a fitting analogy, since it was sea captains on Cape Cod who for the most part in the early nineteenth century first grew cranberries commercially.

"I suppose you'll be busy next week, getting your irrigation system in order."

"Don't remind me," Frank laughed. "It's one of my least favorite tasks." He turned up the collar of his jacket. "Let's get out of this wind."

They strolled around to the rear of the house, where they were sheltered from the wind that ripped across the bog by both the house, and the trees behind it. Between house and trees a stone wall ran down almost to the edge of the bog.

Lena found a relatively flat stone and plunked herself on the low wall. "I imagine this wall is two hundred years old, and was here long before the bog."

Frank nodded. "Part of it was dismantled when they built the bog, maybe a hundred years ago. It continues on the other side of the bog into the swamp."

"Peter Gilbert did a great job of repairing this portion," Lena observed. "If it weren't for these areas still bare of lichen, you'd think it was all original."

"And he did it all at no charge, after he'd finished with the landscaping. I wanted to pay him for his labor but he refused. Said it was always a pleasure to work around a living relic, as he called it, of New England history."

"You know, Frank, I have a hunch," Lena said.

"A hunch?" Frank looked at his companion. "About what? You've already solved the mystery of Peter's death."

Lena shook her head. "Not entirely." She stood up. "My bum's getting cold."

"Let's go inside and crack open that bottle."

"In a bit, Frank." She let her eyes wander along the length of the wall.

"What do you mean by 'not entirely'?"

"I don't like coincidences," Lena replied. "I don't trust them."

"What coincidence are you referring to?"

"That there should be not just one, but two mysteries connected to the Hickman farm. The first: Peter Gilbert and his mysterious death on your road…"

"Which you've cleared up admirably," Frank said.

"And second: the missing treasure."

"Now Lena, you don't really believe such a thing ever existed?"

"If my hunch is right," Lena mused, "it would explain why Peter Gilbert, in his Magic Mushroom-induced state of hallucination, chose to walk down your long lonely driveway in the midst of a violent nor'easter."

"You've lost me," Frank admitted. "I don't see the connection. As far as I can see he was so whacked out by the psychedelic drug that he simply didn't know what he was doing." He paused. "But damn it, you've been right about everything so far, so who am I to argue? What exactly is your hunch?"

"That he had a purpose for coming here."

"What possible purpose?"

Lena pointed to a section of the wall a few yards from where they stood. "I wonder..." she said, more to herself than to Frank. She walked over to the spot she'd indicated, one of the groupings of stone on which the lichen had only just begun to grow.

"This is a bit unusual, isn't it Frank? These three white quartz stones, arranged in a pattern almost like the three balls that designate a pawn broker's shop."

Frank joined her. "It was Peter's idea," he said. "A whim, he told me. I personally don't care for it—it looks too incongruous, not something a Puritan farmer steeped in biblical lore would have done—but Laura felt that it gave the wall 'character.' Besides, Peter wasn't charging us for repairing the wall, so how could I complain."

Lena put her hand against the topmost of the quartz stones. "It feels loose."

"Not an exact fit. I suppose in this instance Peter sacrificed sturdiness for design."

"You don't mind, do you?" Lena asked. Without waiting for an answer she attempted to lift the stone. "Too heavy for me. Can you give me a hand, Frank?"

To humor his friend Frank seized the stone in both hands and lifted it from its position in the wall, then set it on the ground.

The removal of the quartz stone revealed a small cavity in the wall, formed by the unevenness of the stones surrounding it. Lena reached into the cavity and took out a small package wrapped in stiff plastic.

She turned to Frank in triumph. "Fanfare, wild cheers, confetti, and the waving of banners might be appropriate, don't you agree," she said to her stunned companion.

Lena sat in the seat of honor by the Franklin stove. Instead of the promised pinot noir, she held in her hand a flute of brut champagne—her second.

"This calls for the real stuff," Frank had said, even before they unwrapped the package. "I've been saving it for a special occasion. And what could be more special than this?"

Although Frank had been eager to tear into the package right then and there at the stone wall, Lena insisted that they go inside. "These old bones are feeling the cold" —not true; she was flushed with excitement, her body temperature likely in the fever zone— "and besides, I want to do this properly, with the dignity it deserves."

So she marched into the parlor with the package and set it on the coffee table on top of yesterday's newspaper. There, guarded by Lena, it remained until Frank had fetched a knife from the kitchen to cut the cords that bound it.

"The honor of unwrapping it belongs to you," he said.

In the end, throwing all dignity to the dogs, Lena tore into the package with the savage fury of a four-year-old sprawled on the floor under the tree at the crack of dawn on Christmas Day.

Removal of the plastic revealed a metal box, about the size of a small book, which had once held Dorothy Cox chocolates. The box was in pristine shape, as if it had not spent the past seven years tucked into a stone vault exposed to the elements; the plastic had kept it dry.

"Let's hope there are not just chocolates inside," Lena said.

"They'd be a little stale by now," Frank observed.

"Surely Beatrice gobbled them up the minute she received them from Peter," Lena quipped.

"If she has a sweet tooth, it's the only thing sweet about her," Frank said.

Both he and Lena were in a state of nervous tension.

With trembling hands Lena lifted the lid. "Ooo," she said. "Take a gander at these, Frank."

Frank was already peering over her shoulder.

The box contained three pieces of jewelry. Lena lifted them from the box one at a time and laid them out on the coffee table, to one side of the discarded plastic.

A pearl necklace. An emerald bracelet. A diamond brooch.

"All that remains of the loot from Judge Oliver's ransacked mansion," Lena observed. "Pretty, aren't they."

"Exquisite," Frank said. "I know next to nothing about jewelry, but I'd guess these little antique buggers are worth tens of thousands of dollars each. To think that the Hickmans held on to them all those years."

"No doubt because they were the choicest pieces," Lena said. "As each generation culled from the treasure what they needed in order to keep the farm going, they probably began with the coins—gold first, then silver—then the smaller gems."

"You'd think the last of them—what's her name?"

"Molly."

"You'd think she would have sold this lot and used the proceeds to move out of that lonely old farmhouse."

Lena shook her head. "She was a swamp Yankee, Frank—pride in her Puritan ancestry would have run deep. If she was typical, she would have been stubborn and hard as flint. Add to that the fact that she was an old maid, the last of the Hickman line, except for the prodigal brother—whom she expected to return, any day now, if not this year, then next. Year after year, moldering away along with the house and the farm, holding tight to what remained of the treasure—the Hickman legacy—until brother Joe's return."

"And Peter Gilbert found it."

"Where Molly had hidden it, at the base of a stone wall near the house." She shrugged. "Who knows? He might have unearthed it while taking apart one of the walls to obtain the stones to repair yours."

"But why…"

"Why hide it on your property? Remember, Frank: Peter was a hopeless romantic. My guess is that he wanted to save these trinkets for his beloved Beatrice—whom, alas, he knew all too well. He was afraid she'd just sell them, if not for drugs, then for some other frivolity. So he decided to hold onto them until such a time as he felt he could trust her to cherish them."

"She didn't even cherish *him*. She deliberately caused his death." He fondled the necklace, letting the strands of pearls flow through his fingers. "These are rightfully yours, Lena. You figured out where they were hidden."

"Nonsense! What would I do with a bunch of fancy doodads? Keep them, Frank."

"I suppose they would look nice on me," Frank said. "Especially these pearls. I could wear them with my hunting jacket, along with the hip boots I wear when cleaning ditches."

"I'm serious, Frank. I don't want them. You were Peter's friend; he respected you enough to conceal the jewels on your property. Now, wouldn't Laura look nice in those pearls? Surprise her with them on a special occasion—let me know in advance, and I'll send over a brace of champagne bottles. As for the bracelet and brooch—put them in safe deposit, and give them to Maria and Linda when they're grown up enough to appreciate them. You'll have ample time to decide who gets which."

"Lena, how can I ever repay you?"

"Another glass of champagne might do the trick. Followed by a ride home; I'm too tipsy to drive."

The End